Nightmare Detective: The Oracle's Blessing

Nightmare Detective: The Oracle's Blessing

Monk Inyang

Illustrated by
Elijah Isaiah Johnson

SUNTEXT PUBLISHING / NEWARK

Monk Inyang / Suntext Publishing
300 Main St #598
Madison, NJ 07940

www.monkinyang.com

Publisher's Note: This is a work of fiction. Names, characters, places, and incidents are a product of the author's imagination. Locales and public names are sometimes used for atmospheric purposes. Any resemblance to actual people, living or dead, or to businesses, companies, events, institutions, or locales is completely coincidental.

Ordering Information: Special discounts are available on quantity purchases by corporations, associations, and others. For details, contact the publisher at the address above.

Newark / Monk Inyang — First Edition

ISBN 978-1-7325432-2-5

Printed in the United States of America

Chapters

Dear Toni,

I hope you've had an incredible summer. Mine has been so much better than I ever thought it could be. Hanging out with Carlos and Manny has been cool. Femi has been annoying as usual. And my parents have been alright. But the biggest thing has got to be Pangea. You opened a world to me that I can't get enough of. I'm CONSTANTLY jumping in dreams and getting my Nightmare Detective on. It's been dope. And I have you to thank for that.

So, thank you. For everything.

Thanks for the Nightmare Detective training that got me chased by crayon colored dinosaurs, and oversized bees, and Skeletons, and Coyotes, and Chief. It was all worth it because now that I'm a Detective, I feel like I can go wherever I want. And above all that, I got to meet you – the great Toni from Savannah. I wouldn't have done this with anyone but you.

Maybe one day you'll break the rule about not meeting with your recruits and I can tell you this in Pangea. Or even better, I'll be able to tell you this in person. Either way, we're gonna meet again.

That's a promise.

Your boy,
Uko

CHAPTER 1

Welcome to Robeson Middle School

UKO LOOKED BACK at the hulking castle. In this pale moonlight, it looked so imposing. Behind the iron gates, where the four-member team of the best in Pangea awaited Uko's command, lay the castle's entrance. Massive stones lined the winding path leading to the top of the hill on which the castle perched, and floating lanterns cast flickering light on those who dared to enter. Luckily, the rain would mask the team's approach, and the booming thunder would cover the sounds of their tools as they broke in. Everyone just needed to get the go-ahead from Uko.

"I'm not sure," Uko said to Nasir. "Something feels off."

"This is it," Nasir said. His face lit up with each bright flash of lightning, highlighting the long scar that ran the length of his cheek. He was older than Uko and carried himself like a grizzled veteran of unknown wars, yet he looked to him for direction.

"You gave me the opportunity to assemble a team and I did," Nasir continued. "The Gumshoe Detectives were created to get us to this moment." Uko could see the others by the gate grow impatient as they waited for him to make up his mind. "I've been chasing this thing for months. Five of my Gumshoe 1st Class Detectives confirmed the location. You didn't start this war to back away at the end, right?"

Uko wiped the raindrops clouding his vision. He nodded.

"Then let us do our jobs."

Uko looked back at the group waiting at the gate. They crouched expectantly. He knew Nasir was right. He hadn't chased the Coyotes to the corners of Pangea only to be too scared to storm their castle when they discovered it. He couldn't live with himself if he let all of those Detectives die in vain. He turned back to Nasir. "You're right. Let's do it."

Nasir smiled and raised a closed fist to signal the group at the gates. They immediately began cutting a hole into the iron. The plan was in motion.

After a few tense moments, they heard the clank of heavy metal dropping. The group turned back to Nasir and raised a clenched fist. Nasir nodded his approval and pointed toward the castle. The group stealthily climbed through the new hole in the gate.

Nasir glanced at Uko. "You ready?"

Uko did not feel ready at all. He was second-guessing the decision to come this far. It was one thing to defend themselves against the Coyotes. It was another to bring the fight to them. Maybe he shouldn't have let them pull him from his mini-retirement. "What if I said no?"

Nasir chuckled then looked back at the castle. "Let's go, Commander," he said.

Inside the gate, the rain fell heavier on Uko and his group. They stood in silence while taking in their new surroundings.

"They probably have surveillance along the path," Nasir whispered. "It took so long to disable the gate's camera that it would be a waste of time to do that to any others. We just have to avoid them."

2

"There are some stairs back there," Uko said. He pointed at some moss-covered cobblestones that were hidden by the trunk of a massive tree. They led straight up toward the castle.

Nasir clapped him on the back. "Excellent. Good eye. Mel, head up the stairs. Scout for traps or cameras. Bronson, go with her. We'll see if there's anything of interest around here."

A tall woman in the group quietly nodded and dashed to the stairs. A hulking man in all black followed closely behind her. Nasir and two others remained with Uko. They spoke quietly with each other as they weighed their next options. Nasir knelt by Uko and dug through his bookbag in search of something.
"I need to keep this more organized," Nasir said to himself. Uko looked from him to the path in front of the group. The trees cast dark shadows that made it hard to see farther than a few feet. As Uko stared, and thunder rumbled, a flash of lightning illuminated the road ahead. Uko could see the silhouette of what looked like an oversized dog walking toward them. A lump formed in his throat, and he pointed a shaky finger in its direction. Nasir looked up from his bag, his eyes following the direction of Uko's finger. At that moment, another flash of light highlighted the animal again as it sniffed the ground and continued toward them. Nasir immediately dropped his bag, pulled the walkie-talkie from his hip, and brought it to his mouth.

"We got a sighting. Knuckle up," he whispered into it.

"Where do you see the Coyote?" a woman's voice crackled back in response.

"Right in front of us at the base of the path," Nasir replied. Uko's head swiveled from side to side as he tried to decide what he should do.

"Well, that came fast," the woman replied. "This is it."

Nasir looked back at a frightened Uko and smiled. He put the walkie to his mouth and held the button down to speak again. "Yes, it is. Godspeed."

◆ ◆ ◆

THREE MONTHS EARLIER

◆ ◆ ◆

"Attention students, please remember our back-to-school night assembly is this Thursday at 6:30 PM."

The sound of a tired voice droned through the loudspeaker above Uko's head as he sat at his desk. It sighed and continued, "If your parents are attending, they must bring their ten dollar donation to the Robeson Middle School PTA. Also, whoever left gum on the announcement desk's seat today, this is a warning. An investigation is already underway. You will be dealt with swiftly. If you wish to turn yourself in, please speak to your homeroom teacher. Have a litty day."

Uko exchanged glances with Manny at the desk next to him. They laughed to themselves.

A lanky boy in a dingy hoodie behind Manny leaned forward in his desk and tapped him on the shoulder.

"Was it you two?" he asked.

"No," Manny said.

"Boo," the boy said as he sat back. "Y'all corny."

Manny looked at Uko, confused. "Okay, I guess."

The classroom was filled with 25 sixth graders in individual school desks. Some spoke loudly, some laughed at jokes from others around them, and some slept. Uko and Manny were the only two who were awake and quiet. Even though everyone else knew each other from their neighborhoods and elementary schools, Uko and Manny didn't know anyone but each other. It was early in the new school year, but meeting friends in middle school felt like moving mountains. Cliques had been formed on day one, but Manny and Uko had missed the boat.

"You and your folks coming to back-to-school night?" Uko asked Manny.

Manny rested his head on his desk. "What choice do I have?"

"Yeah, you're right." Uko looked around at the classroom to watch groups of kids in deep conversations about their weekends. Manny and Uko had spent their weekend hanging out together, so there was nothing to discuss.

Manny glanced at Uko. "We just gotta put ourselves out there, bro."

"What are you talking about?" Uko replied.

"If we're gonna survive the school year without dying of boredom, we're gonna need new friends," Manny said. "That means talking to people other than each other." He motioned to the rest of the class as another group erupted into loud laughter.

"I think we're good," Uko said.

"No, we're not. Two weeks into the new school year and we barely know the names of the kids in homeroom. We already ran out of stuff to talk about."

"That's not true," Uko said as he searched his mind for a new topic.

"Oh yeah? Go ahead."

"Okay, gimme a second," Uko said.

"I swear if it's what I think it is, I'm done with you till lunch. You'll be on timeout."

"You don't know what it is," Uko said as the bell to end homeroom rung.

"Does it have something to do with being this close to finding Toni?" Manny said as he stood up and gathered his things.

"Huh?" Uko asked, though they both knew he'd heard him clearly.

"I knew it," Manny said. "We're done till lunch. You sittin' here wasting my time." He began walking out of the class with the rest of the kids.

Uko laughed and ran to meet him. "All right, Manny, I'll see you in third period."

"Manny and Uko, can you boys come here for a moment?" Ms. Givens, their homeroom teacher, called out to them from her desk in front of the class. Both boys turned back to her in confusion. "You're not in trouble," she added. "I just wanted to speak to you guys about something."

Uko and Manny walked back to Ms. Givens' desk as the room emptied out. She waited until it was completely clear before speaking, her eyes full of concern.

"How you guys holding up so far?"

"We're good," Uko said automatically.

"Are you?" Ms. Givens asked as she looked at Manny. "I see you two are pretty much keeping to yourselves."

"We're just getting used to everything," Manny replied. "Everyone already knows each other, so it's kinda tough."

"Yeah, I get it," Ms. Givens said. "Have you looked into joining a club? Or playing a sport?"

"I don't know, Ms. Givens. I think we're fine the way things are," Uko said.

"How about basketball or bowling?" Ms. Givens asked. They both shook their heads no.

"You can join the debate team or Robotics Club," she added.

"Trash," Uko replied.

"Come on, Uko," Ms. Givens said. "You gotta give something a chance. What about Chess Club or Coding Club?"

"What's Coding Club?" Uko asked. "Do they code apps?"

"Kind of," Ms. Givens replied. "They actually create video games. You learn some coding so you can make your own. Some of the kids made Pac-Man last year." She looked at the growing smiles on Uko's and Manny's faces. "I'm guessing I might have hit the jackpot with that one?"

"I mean, we can check it out. See what it's lookin' like," Uko said to Manny.

Manny shrugged. "I guess. When's the next meeting?"

Ms. Givens clapped her hands in excitement. "They meet today at 3:30 in the computer room. You guys will love it. Now get to your next class. If you're late, I'm not going to be your alibi."

As Uko sat through the rest of his classes that day, all he could think about was Coding Club. When the final bell rang, he ran to his locker to put his books away and wait for Manny. But when he arrived, Manny was already there and ready to go.

"I'm guessing you're excited about CC too," Uko said.

"What's CC?"

"Coding Club," Uko replied.

"Look at you. Already got nicknames," Manny said.

They both walked through halls filled with kids rushing in random directions on their way to the computer lab in Room 55. On the door, a handwritten sign read, "Coding Club: Beware of Dog." Below the title, someone drew a chihuahua with the words "Like this? lol" below it. Uko looked over to Manny, who simply shook his head.

Inside the room were five rows of desks with computer monitors on each. In the first row, three kids huddled around a single monitor. Two rows behind them, another group of three kids were bunched around another monitor with a woman standing over them. When Manny and Uko walked in, she was the only person to look up. She slowly waddled over with an annoyed expression. "Who are you two?"

"I'm Uko, and this is Manny."

"What do you want?"

"Is this Coding Club?" Manny asked.

"Yes," she replied shortly. They all stared at each other in silence.

"Can we join?" Uko asked. He tried to ignore how weird she was making this.

The teacher looked back at the group she was with before they interrupted her. When she turned back to Uko and Manny, she sighed heavily.

"What do you know about computers or making video games?" she asked.

"Uh, I haven't really done anything like this before," Uko answered with hesitation. "Our homeroom teacher Ms. Givens said we should join to make new friends."

She looked from Uko to Manny. "So you're nerds."

"I wouldn't say all that," Manny protested. "We just don't know anyone."

"Sure. My name is Ms. Kowalski. This is the group. We meet every Monday and Thursday afternoon from 3:30 to 5:30. I cut out the lights and walk out that door at 5:30 on the dot. You might think I'm joking, but I'll be in my car by 5:32. You understand?"

"Yes," Uko said.

"Have a seat by him." Ms. Kowalski pointed to a small boy hunched behind a monitor in the last row. Uko was surprised he hadn't noticed him when they first walked in. "He's new too. He can show you how to get to the intro video." She immediately walked back to the group she was with before. The two girls and boy in the group never looked up.

"Do you wanna just go?" Manny asked.

"Let's just give it a shot. Maybe this kid in the back is cool," Uko said. He was trying to convince himself more than he was Manny.

"Ugh," Manny said. "Fine, let's go back there. If he's weird too, then I'm out."

9

"Cool," Uko replied. They walked to the back of the room and sat near the boy.

"What's up?" Uko said. "My name is Uko, and this is Manny."

"Yeah, I heard when you guys first came in," he said. "I'm Brandon."

"Does she always act like that?"

Brandon laughed and nodded his head. "She's weird, right?"

"Yes!" Uko and Manny said at the same time.

"She's like that. This is my third day here and she hasn't paid me any mind other than telling me to watch the 'Intro to Gaming Video.' I finished that my first day," Brandon replied.

"So, what are you doing now?" Uko asked.

The boy sized Uko and Manny up. Finally, he turned back to his computer and opened an internet browser with a blog loaded.

"I'm watching," Brandon replied. "And I'm writing."

Uko and Manny exchanged more confused looks.

"What are you writing?" Manny asked.

"Have you ever heard of the blog 'Last Word?'" Brandon asked without looking away from the monitor.

"No." Uko looked at Manny.

"No, me neither," Manny added.

"It's where you can find out about what's going on in the school, written by students who go here. Sorta like school newspapers from back in the day," Brandon said. "But it's underground and everyone on it is anonymous. That way we can be real."

"So, you come to Coding Club and blog about the school?" Uko asked. "Can't you just use your own laptop at home or something?"

"I come to Coding Club because I'm writing about Ms. Kowalski. She's doing something illegal here," Brandon said quietly. "And I plan on being the one to catch her."

CHAPTER 2

Trust Your Nobility

UKO STARED AT BRANDON in shock.

Manny threw his hands up. "What? Are you serious?"

"Absolutely," Brandon said. "I can't prove anything right now other than the fact that she's crazy mean. But I'm pretty sure she's cooking something up here."

Uko crossed his arms. "What makes you think that?"

Brandon leaned closer to them. "I got a tip from one of our CIs about her."

"What's a CI?" Manny asked.

"Confidential Informant," Brandon replied with a face that suggested the question was ridiculous. Uko rolled his eyes.

"My CI told me that she tried to join the group, but Ms. Kowalski gave her a really hard time about it. She kept asking her all these questions about computers. Really tough questions. My CI answers all of them perfectly, cuz she knows her stuff. Ms. Kowalski tells her she can't join and comes up with some dumb excuse about it being full." Brandon pointed to the group of six students at the front of the computer lab, with more than 25 computers still available. "At that time, there were two less people in the room than you see up front there now."

Uko glanced over at Manny's intrigued expression. They were both hanging on every word.

"So my CI follows up with Vice Principal Mallard, and he's really weird about the whole thing and doesn't give her any straight answers. Then she finds out Justin and Sheena got into the club a week after she tried. They might be two of the dumbest eighth graders in the whole school," Brandon said. "So now she's really confused. That's when she reached out to the blog. Which brings me here now."

Uko sat back in disbelief. "What do you think Ms. Kowalski is doing?"

"Not sure. But I'll find out."

"How?" Manny asked.

"That's the problem. I'm the only kid who's joined since we got the tip. If I find something and then write about it on Last Word, they might put two and two together and figure out my pen name. This could all be a setup to find out our real identities—see if we take the bait. Can't have that."

"It can't be this serious, my guy," Manny said.

"It definitely is," Brandon coolly replied. "Everybody in this school reads Last Word. We've gotten three kids expelled and two teachers put on probation with the district. We wrote about the eighth grade prom scandal last year, and it was on the local news." Brandon lowered his voice again after seeing Ms. Kowalski turn back to look at them for a brief second. "Down at City Hall, they read everything we post within the hour. People want to know who we are. It wouldn't be good for any of us if that happens."

Uko was fascinated. It was crazy to think a group of unseen students had that much power.

"But now you two joined," Brandon continued. "If I figure out the secret now and write about it, then they won't know who wrote it. And if you're interested, you could be sources. WE could crack this thing together."

"How would we find out?" Uko asked. He was pretty much sold on the idea. The original plan of meeting a bunch of potential friends sounded good in theory. But that's a lot of work. Uko loved writing, and thought being an anonymous blogger on a site that the entire school read sounded way more appealing.

Manny spun on Uko. "Are you serious? We were just supposed to meet a few people and code Minecraft or something."

"You'd go undercover," Brandon said, ignoring Manny. "I'd coach you through asking the right questions without getting caught. I've done it a few times before."

"You have people go undercover all the time, I'm guessing," Manny said. "Real serious crime fighting work you're doing."

"Prom Apocalypse was a big deal!"

"All right guys, calm down," Uko said, glancing at the front of the room.

"This is real," Brandon whispered to Uko. "Your boy might not believe me, but there's something going on here. Me and the team are gonna figure it out either way. I'm giving you guys a shot to be a part of that."

Uko looked at Manny, who stared back at him expressionless. Uko desperately wanted to shake up the ordinary "show-up-then-go-home" school routine he and Manny had been in. Being able to follow Brandon's lead in that shakeup made it even better. They could join the ride without having to be front and center—just the way Uko liked it.

"What do you think?" Uko asked.

Manny looked to his monitor and shook his head in silence for a moment. "I don't know."

"You were never going to learn how to code Minecraft," Brandon added.

"It's up to you, Uko," Manny said. "If you're down, then we'll figure it out." Uko loved being able to count on the loyalty of his best friend.

Brandon turned to Uko. "What do ya wanna do?"

The room suddenly went dark, the bright computer monitors the only thing providing light. Ms. Kowalski's voice boomed from the front of the room.

"It's 5:29," she said with annoyance. "Everybody get out!"

Everyone in the room stood up and began packing their things in the dark, since Ms. Kowalski never turned the lights back on after her announcement.

"Think about it," Brandon said to Uko after slinging on his bookbag. "I'll talk to you tomorrow."

"Where?" Manny asked.

"I'll find you," he replied before walking past Ms. Kowalski and out of the room.

Uko and Manny exited the building and began heading back home. It was the type of warm, early September day in Newark that reminded you of the summer that just passed. They took in the sights and sounds of the bustling city while colored leaves crunched under their feet.

"How do you feel about working on that story for Last Word?" Uko asked again.

"How do we even know if it's the big deal he says it is?"

"Right." As they crossed the street onto another block, Uko waited for Manny to elaborate. He never did. The silence annoyed Uko, who had a million thoughts about the information they had just heard. As they reached the store Caribbean Grilled, Manny finally spoke. "I'm gonna get a beef patty. You want one?"

"I'm good," Uko replied. "I'll just wait out here."

Manny patted his jeans pockets. "How much does a patty with cheese cost?" He pulled a single dollar from his pocket. "It's a dollar, right?"

"You've been here a million times. It's two," Uko replied. He dug in his pocket and handed Manny another bill.

Manny walked into the store while Uko paced outside. The thought of Ms. Kowalski being involved in something illegal and a student being the one to catch her ran through his mind. If it was true, should he tell someone like the principal or another teacher? Would they even believe him? What if he helped Brandon and got caught? By the time Manny came out of the store with his patty in hand, Uko jumped into the conversation he was having in his head.

"We could easily just go to school every day, keep to ourselves, and have a calm, quiet year," Uko blurted out. "Or we can see how this thing with Brandon goes and do something exciting."

"Oh yeah?" Manny asked between bites.

"Yeah, and that blog looked legit. If he writes for them, then he's probably connected to some interesting people."

"Makes sense," Manny said with a mouth full of patty. "That prom thing he spoke about was def a big deal when it happened."

"If we link up with him...wait, what did you say? You knew about the prom thing?"

"Yup."

"How?"

"I heard some kids talk about the blog in my art class today. I looked it up on my phone during lunch and read a bunch of articles. It's good stuff. Wild comments," Manny said with a sly smile.

"When he asked if we heard about it, why did you say no?" Uko asked.

"Play dumb from time to time," Manny replied. "You'd be surprised what you get when people think you don't know what they're talking about." He reached in his pocket and pulled out an extra dollar bill. Uko stared at him before laughing, and reached out to take back his dollar. Manny pulled away and put it back in his pocket. "Nope! I'm using this to get something to drink later."

"I hate you," Uko said.

"You mad?"

The boys said goodbye to each other as they arrived at Manny's house. Uko walked another three doors down the block to his own house. He paused at his door, gazing at the park across the street. The sounds of kids laughing as they ran around made him miss summer even more. As he stared at the entrance to the park, he remembered the dream that had haunted him through most of last summer. He remembered running there in his nightmare. He could see a vision of himself standing there with Toni by his side. She silently laughed and pointed at him and the house.

As he placed his key into the lock, the door was yanked open from the other side. His dad nearly ran into him as he hustled out of the house.

"Sorry, Coco," he said. "How was school?"

"It was fine," Uko replied as his dad slid by him, dressed in his red and black tracksuit. "How was work?"

"Same," his dad replied as he got to the street. "I gotta get this run in before dinner. Otherwise I won't do it. I'll see you when I get back, Coco." He began briskly jogging down the block.

"Uko!" Femi called to him from inside the house. "Settle this debate." Uko's older brother Femi and his mother looked at him expectantly from the living room.

"Femi is over here blaspheming," Uko's mom yelled as he closed the door behind him. "I'm assuming you have some kind of sense."

"Mom thinks *Sister Act II* is a better movie than *Black Panther*," Femi yelled out while laughing. "Tell her she's crazy."

Uko was both caught off guard by the question and amused by the intensity of the argument. He continued up the stairs to his room.

"Neither of them were as good as *John Q*," he said before disappearing. The room below him erupted in disagreement. Uko chuckled to himself as he reached the second floor and slipped into his room. He looked over to his dresser and said hello to the stuffed lion he acknowledged each day he returned home. "What's up, Kanju?"

He tossed his bookbag to the side and plopped on his bed face down. His body relaxed as the weight of a long day escaped with each breath. He immediately drifted into an unexpected nap.

Kanju and his calm bedroom disappeared. He was suddenly in the backseat of his dad's parked SUV as the entire family stood outside of it, staring at him with annoyance.

"Coco!" his mother yelled. "Let's go! What are you doing?"

Uko unbuckled his seatbelt while trying to understand where he was. The neighborhood they were now parked in was unfamiliar. As his parents looked back at him from the street outside the car, Uko scanned the block for signs that would help ground him.

"Where are we?" Uko asked as he stepped out of the car.

"Brooklyn," Femi replied. "How many times we gonna have to say it?"

Uko looked at his brother in surprise. For a moment, he was worried that his mind had somehow failed him. The slight blurriness of his brother's face clued him to the real explanation—he was in a dream.

"What are we doing here?" Uko asked.

"You're preaching to the choir, bro," Femi replied. "I don't believe in this crazy stuff either. Prophets? Really?"

"What?" They waited for a car to pass them before continuing to cross the street.

"You're going first," Femi replied with a grin. "And I'm gonna record it."

When they reached the sidewalk, their dad held the door of a small store open and waved them in. The store was a tight space filled with random items on sparse shelves. Uko saw bags of rice and assorted canned foods next to religious candles and old books. In the back of the store was a small desk with an old-fashioned register and no one standing behind it. The lack of windows meant the room was only illuminated by a single fluorescent light bulb that swung above them.

Uko's mom walked to the desk and apprehensively tapped the bell resting on it. They waited in silence for what felt like several minutes. Finally, a thin man who looked to be in his seventies walked out to the desk. He looked at the family in silence.

"Hello," Uko's dad said. The man didn't reply. "We're here to see Shep."

The man held out a hand. Uko's dad placed a roll of cash into it. Without speaking or looking at the money, the man turned around and walked out of the door he appeared from.

"Do we follow him?" Uko's mom asked.

"I don't even know what's happening," Uko replied.

Before anyone could speak again, the man opened the door wide. "Come," he said in a gruff voice. The family exchanged glances and followed the man into the much smaller backroom. The clutter stacked high against the walls pressed in on them. There was only enough room for Uko, the old man who walked them in, and another man who sat on a folding chair in the center of the room.

"They're here to see you, Shep," the old man said to the guy on the chair.

"I have time for one," Shep replied. He stared at the Hill family cramped in the doorway. "You," he said, pointing at an uncomfortable Uko.

Uko's eyes darted from Shep to the old man, then to his family standing behind him. *What the heck is going on? What's he gonna do to me?* His parents returned his concerned looks with forced smiles. He noticed Femi in the back of the group with his cellphone raised to record the occasion.

"Thank you, Shep," Uko's dad said. "Can we stay here while you read his future?"

"No one can tell the future," Shep replied without taking his eyes off of Uko. "I can tell you what I see for the boy. It's up to him to fulfill it."

"Okay. That works," Uko's dad replied, pushing Uko closer.

Shep held out his hands to Uko. He looked down at them, unsure what to do.

"Why are you frightened?" Shep asked. "I'm not going to harm you." For the first time, he looked inviting. He took Uko's hands into his and stared at his sweaty palms.

"Such a young child," Shep said quietly to himself. "Who's seen so much." He looked up into Uko's eyes. Uko's worry slowly transformed into curiosity. What would this mysterious man say?

"Incredible," Shep continued. "This boy is a warrior."

Femi laughed loudly from the back. Everyone shot him a look and he snapped his mouth shut.

Shep looked back to Uko and let go of his hands. "You have been blessed with the gift of sight through closed eyes. It must be taken solemnly and seriously. You've also been given a heavy burden. One I'm not sure you can handle."

Uko's curiosity faded, fear returning in its wake.

"I see masses standing behind you. You will be a leader of these people. They believe in you and will fight for you—this army," Shep said gravely. He turned to Uko's parents. "The burdens of a leader are heavy indeed. Guide him. Trust your nobility," he added before closing his eyes.

"He's finished," the old man said. He raised his hand to guide them back out of the room. Femi put his phone away, disappointed, and their parents trickled out after him. As Uko turned for the door, Shep suddenly reached out and grabbed his arm tightly.

"Beware," Shep said gravely. "Your enemies hold you in ill regard."

He let go of Uko's arm, leaving an imprint where he gripped it.

"Uko! What are you doing?! Come downstairs!" Uko's mom screamed from downstairs. "We're not waiting forever to start dinner."

Suddenly Uko was back in his room, in the same clothes he'd worn to school and his bookbag on the floor next to him. Shep's words echoed in his head.

They believe in you and will fight for you—this army.

How on Earth would an army of people fight for HIM? He'd never thought of himself as some flashy leader. This had to be a case of mistaken identity.

"Uko!" his mom yelled again from downstairs.

"I'm coming, Mommy."

CHAPTER 3

Detective Light Work

AFTER DINNER, Uko returned to his room and plopped back on his bed. He stared at his messy dresser while trying to figure out what he should think of his brief dream earlier. He'd never had such an intense dream during a nap. He couldn't have been asleep for that long, yet everything seemed so vivid. It felt like he was really there with his family in a cramped store in Brooklyn.

"Your foes hold you in ill regard," Uko said out loud to Kanju.

Kanju responded with silence.

He turned out the lights and got into bed. Even though that last trip still confused him, one thing Uko was comfortable with was his time in Pangea. He figured he'd go to sleep, solve some nightmares, and somehow figure it all out when he woke up.

"G'night, Kanju." He closed his eyes and drifted to his happy place.

❖ ❖ ❖

Uko stood up from the log he sat on in the serene meadow. He was back for another day at the office. He swung his arms back and forth in front of him, stretched his back, and bent over to touch his toes. He took a deep breath,

25

taking in the lush green grass under his feet and the bright blue sky above his head.

"Is everybody ready?" he said to himself. "Then let's go."

He sprinted to the thick patch of trees at the edge of the meadow—toward the Silk Road he knew so well. He skipped past the treeline and into the darkening path with arms held wide open to high-five the mossy tree trunks. Even before the road became too dark for him to see things clearly, he closed his eyes and navigated the winding path with intuition alone. He picked up speed. There was nothing that compared to this. The feeling of being in complete control and in his element was exhilarating. When he finally reached the fork in the road where his DreamHub would always appear, he capped off his run with an enthusiastic cartwheel. The familiar colorful silver and purple mist poured down from above as he dusted dirt from his hands. The mist thickened to a fog that swirled in front of him.

"What's on deck tonight?"

He put his hands to his chin and surveyed the flickering images that danced before him. He was much better at interpreting what he saw. Things were grainy, but he could make out the outlines of trains barreling from one purple cloud into another. He could make out hundreds of people moving in different directions. He liked staring at a person as they took the form of a stray wisp a few inches in front of everyone else. After a couple of seconds their image would disappear, and he'd look for something else to focus on. Tonight, he zeroed in on the image of a person creeping forward as if they were hiding. Uko walked over to the wisp and reached out to it. It swirled around his finger.

"I got you," he said, as the bright light flashed and everything around him became white.

❖ ❖ ❖

"Diana!"

The yell was the first thing he heard as the bright flash began to recede. To his surprise, it looked like he was still in the same forest of a second before.

"Yo! Where are you guys?" the voice yelled out again.

Uko's eyes finally settled, and he was able to take in his surroundings. He looked up to the sky and saw the light from a full moon filtering down through the leaves and branches overhead. He was not in the pitch-black clearing lit by the DreamHub.

"I don't know where I'm supposed to go," the voice said.

Uko whipped his head in the direction of the voice and began walking toward it. He was careful to make as little noise as possible as he approached, wanting to get a clear idea of everything he was about to encounter. A few nights ago he made the mistake of rushing in, and ended up face-to-face with a burglar as she crept through his client's house. Since then, he made sure to take in his surroundings before announcing his presence.

As he silently cleared a group of dead branches, he saw a frantic looking boy standing in a campsite. There were empty tents, a dying fire, and supplies that were spilled in random directions. Uko stood behind a tree and observed the boy as he walked back and forth in a fruitless search for something. After a few moments, Uko called out to him, stepping out from behind the tree.

"Kev, are you all right?" he asked.

The boy's head darted up, and he jumped back in surprise.

27

"How do you know my name?"

Uko pointed to a neon orange name badge on the boy's arm. "Your name's on your arm. My name's Uko," he said as he continued to walk toward him.

The boy looked around as if he expected someone to help him. "Do you know where everyone is?"

"Nope," Uko said matter-of-factly. "But I can help you find them."

"How?" Kevin asked, zipping up his neon jacket.

"You won't believe me," Uko replied. "But you're in a dream, buddy."

"What?"

"Nightmare. Excuse me."

"What?"

"We're off to a great start." Uko chuckled. He pointed to a tree at the end of the campsite. "Do you see that neon green thing hanging from the branch?"

Kevin nodded as he spotted it. "Yeah."

"Looks like the same color of your jacket," Uko said. "Were you all wearing the same jackets?"

"Yeah, we were."

"Thought so. Let's go that way then."

The boys walked toward the strip of jacket and into the woods. Uko swiped it up as he passed and stared at it as he made conversation with Kevin.

"So what were you guys doing?"

"Senior year camping trip. It's supposed to be a bonding experience before we leave for the summer and then go to college."

Uko looked around. "So this is springtime? What month is it?"

Kevin looked at him like he was crazy. "April."

"Got it. And where are we?"

"Mountain State Park."

"Oh yeah? Where is that?"

Kevin stared at him for a few seconds before answering. "Georgia. Who did you say you were again? And what are you doing here?"

"Georgia," Uko repeated with intrigue. "Are we close to Savannah?"

"No. Savannah's like five hours away," Kevin stopped walking. "You didn't answer my question."

Uko squatted to get a closer look at something he found on the ground. He turned back to Kevin who had stopped walking. "My bad. What did you say again?"

Before Kevin could repeat his question, the sound of cracking branches to their left interrupted them. Both boys stood at attention, searching. Kevin walked over to Uko and as he reached him, the silhouette of what looked like a massive oversized cat appeared from behind a large rock. The silhouette stalked closer until the moonlight illuminated its features. It was much larger than it looked in the shadows, close to the size of a small horse. Its light brown fur was flawless; it rippled with each deep purr as it stood incredibly still.

"Oh my God," Kevin whispered.

"What is that?" Uko asked, a little worry in his voice.

"How am I supposed to know?! It's probably a freaking lion or something."

"Nah. I don't think that's a lion," Uko said as he began to back up. As he did, he gently pulled Kevin's arm to let him know to do the same.

The massive cat responded to this retreat by bowing its head and lowering the front of its body to the ground, keeping eye contact with the boys the entire time. When they continued to back up, it trotted a few feet forward and repeated the gesture. Uko stopped moving.

"What are you doing?" Kevin asked.

"Hold up. You see what it's doing?" Uko asked while pointing to the cat.

"Yeah, it's probably gonna pounce on us. Let's go!"

"No, look at its face."

Its eyes were big and inviting like the eyes of a cartoon kitten. Its lips curled upward. It was smiling. Uko stepped forward with his hand out, ignoring Kevin's tugs at his shirt. The cat's purr grew stronger.

"Are you trying to get killed?!"

"I don't think it wants to hurt us. I think it's friendly." Uko walked closer to the cat while keeping his hand out. "Hey, kitty. How are you doing tonight?"

"Stop!" Kevin screamed.

The cat lowered its head at Uko's outstretched hand. He held his breath, attempting to keep calm now that he was this close. In the moment of truth, the cat allowed Uko to pet him, purring loudly when he did. It raised its head and walked around him, brushing itself against his shirt and nearly pushing him down with the movement.

"Come pet it," Uko said. Kevin shook his head and backed up farther. "Come on, it's friendly."

Kevin froze and glanced at Uko apprehensively. Before he could move, the cat left Uko's side and trotted over. He screamed and turned to run, but the cat's long strides closed the distance between them instantly. Before he could react, the cat was purring and rubbing itself on Kevin, who was immediately knocked down. Uko laughed as Kevin got to his feet, gingerly brushing his fingers along the cat's fur.

"I was right," he said as he watched it carefully. "It's a mountain lion."

"Really?" Uko replied. "That's crazy." He walked over to Kevin and pointed in the direction they were originally walking. "Let's keep going so we can find your people."

As Kevin began walking, the lion walked in front of him and blocked his way. He attempted to walk around it and it did the same thing.

"What is it doing?" Kevin asked.

"Not sure."

Kevin backed up and tried to go around the lion again and was blocked another time. He tried walking in the opposite direction, toward where the lion appeared. It stopped trying to block him and happily walked alongside him. Kevin noticed this and tried to turn back toward Uko. He was stopped again.

"I guess we're walking this way now," Kevin said as he pointed back to the thick patch of trees.

"Yeah, I guess so."

The lion moved quickly, and the boys struggled to follow, ducking underneath low branches and clearing the numerous fallen tree trunks. After a few moments of excited dashing, they eventually caught up to the beast just as it stopped to paw the ground. It resumed its loud purr, circling the boys again. Uko looked around for the next clue. If he could find it quickly, it would help lead his client to solving the nightmare before things took a turn for the worse. The area looked like the rest of the woods that they'd run from. The grass and trees all looked the same.

"So what do we do now?" Kevin asked, looking around nervously.

"Not sure. Do you see anything that could give us a clue?"

"No," Kevin replied. "I hate being out here by myself. I feel like something's gonna happen."

As he spoke, Kevin wiped something from his hair. Even though Kevin wasn't aware, Uko noticed its metallic color glinting in the moonlight as it fell to the ground. He walked over to inspect it.

"I think we should just leave," Kevin said as he noticed Uko staring at the ground. "What do you think?"

Uko didn't reply. Instead he squatted down and picked up something from the grass. It was shiny on one side and had a colorful design on the other.

From the design, Uko could tell it was ripped from something larger. He held it out to Kevin.

"What is this, Kev?"

Kevin took it from Uko's hand and inspected it. "A candy wrapper."

"Yup," Uko replied.

"So what's the big deal about a candy wrapper?" The lion walked over and licked the wrapper in Kevin's hand. He pulled away with a shriek at the brush of its heavy, wet tongue.

"Aren't we in the middle of nowhere?" Uko asked. "What's a candy wrapper doing out here?"

"Somebody probably camped here before. What's so special about that?"

"Yeah, but there's something weird about this one," Uko said as he straightened up and pointed to the ground with his shoe. "That one wasn't on the ground a few seconds ago. It fell down onto your hair and you brushed it off."

Kevin stared at Uko. "Okay, so what?"

"So candy wrappers just fall from the sky now?" Uko patiently asked.

Kevin furrowed his brow.

Uko pulled him to the spot where the wrapper fell and pointed to the tree branches above them. "Look up there."

On a tree branch several feet above them, a girl in a puffy bubble jacket swung her feet as she stared down at them. Next to her was another girl chomping on a candy bar and laughing quietly. As Uko looked farther up into the trees, he saw more and more kids on different branches. They all burst out into loud laughter when Kevin noticed them and said, "Oh, there you guys are." He looked back at Uko, and with a sigh of relief asked, "How did you figure that out?"

"It's what I do. Keep looking for things and they always show up."

"Cool. Thank you," Kevin said as he and the woods around them began to fade to white. The last thing Uko heard was the distant sound of Kevin yelling, "This ain't funny. I hope all y'all fall."

The soft woosh and deep purple colors of Uko's DreamHub appeared in front of him as the woods and Kevin's voice faded away.

Uko walked over to the trunk of a tree directly next to the sheet of clouds. In the light of the DreamHub, Uko counted the numerous tally marks on the tree's side.

"Seventy-three. That's what you call a successful summer," he said to himself. "A seventy-three case summer. I could probably double that by Christmas."

He swung back to the DreamHub, closed his eyes, and reached out blindly. The woosh grew louder as a new gust of vapor wrapped around him.

"Surprise me."

CHAPTER 4

Gifts from Nana

THE BANG OF DAZZLING WHITE LIGHT crept in through Uko's closed eyes.

"Move," a deep voice yelled out. As Uko opened his eyes, he saw that the command came from a large man standing behind him.

"What's wrong with you? Are you deaf? Move!"

Uko scanned the tight hallway where they stood. The concrete walls were plastered end to end with posters, each one with flashy titles that flickered and changed in size randomly as you gazed at them.

FIGHT NIGHT!!!! Cummings vs Jenkins II - The Rematch

Ramos vs Carrington - Friday the 13th: The Funeral Fight

Ladies' Fight Night!! Ampomah vs Jung - The International Incident

Under each title were pictures of sweaty-looking people with boxing gloves as they stared at each other in fighting stances. Some were brand new and huge, while others were yellowing with age and tiny in comparison. Uko's eyes jumped from poster to poster as he whirled around.

"Are you lost or are you just dumb?" the man yelled out. There was a crowd behind him that Uko didn't see before he burst out into laughter.

"I'm good."

"So walk inside, 'lil man! I'm hungry and you're wasting my time."

Uko strode down the hall, the man following closely behind. He continued scanning the wall, full of men and women he had never heard of. Every time Uko read a poster's title, it immediately slid to the ground.

Locklear vs Yazzie: The Snazzy Situation

Begay vs Polat: The Turkey Thanksgiving

Temples vs Garner: Garden Variety Combat

After a few moments, Uko and the group behind him made it to a ten-foot-tall black steel door.

"Knock," the man behind Uko ordered. "Come on now. You act like you've never been here before."

Though frustrated, Uko knew better than to express it right now while he was so outnumbered. He took a deep breath and knocked. Suddenly, a window slid open at eye level. A face hidden in shadows pressed against the small window.

"Password."

Uko glanced at the impatient man behind him.

"Banana bread," the man barked.

The loud clack of locks opening echoed in the hallway. Finally, the door swung open to reveal a bustling room.

"What is this place?" Uko asked the man as he pushed past him.

He shot him an irritated look. "Lucky Death, 'lil man. Keep up," he said as he walked away.

The rest of the group crowded in. People were laughing, drinking and eating throughout the dimly lit room. Small dinner tables surrounded a tiny stage where a woman with a black feather boa sang into a microphone. Behind the tables was a bar, where even more people sat on stools. Waiters, bartenders and patrons dashed around in all directions. The smoke-filled room was so busy with music and activity that everything seemed to be vibrating.

Spotting an empty stool at the bar in the back of the room, Uko took a seat. He figured it'd be a good vantage point from up there.

"What you having, darling?" asked the bartender.

Uko looked over his shoulder and shook his head no. "Sorry, I don't drink."

"Why not?"

Uko's brow furrowed. He thought it was pretty obvious.

"Because I'm twelve."

"Then why are you here?" the bartender asked. Valid question. Uko couldn't even think of a good response.

"He'll have a ginger ale and pine," his neighbor ordered. It was the same man from the hallway. "You here to help me with my nightmare, 'lil man?" he said.

Uko's eyes widened.

"My name's Charles. My people call me Slim." He extended a hulking hand that dwarfed Uko's. "Funny, right?"

"Yeah," Uko said, a little stunned. "How did you know about me?"

"Look around." Slim pointed down the bar and at the tables surrounding the stage. "You see any kids in here?"

Uko scanned the room. Eerily, as he looked at people, each would return his glance with a stare, as if they felt him look their way. He shuddered and quickly looked back at Slim.

"No."

"Exactly. You stood out the second you came into that hallway," Slim said. "I was just giving you a hard time to see if you'd run away. I'm surprised you didn't."

The bartender placed a tall glass with brown liquid in front of Uko.

"I'm paying for your drinks. You better be good at your job," Slim said. Uko stared at the glass with apprehension. "It's okay, it's just ginger ale and pine." Slim added.

"What's pine?"

"It's like a syrup. They make it from pinecones. You'll like it."

Uko didn't think he would but didn't know how to politely decline. Instead he picked up the glass and took a small sip. Its bittersweet taste was a pleasant surprise.

"So how long have you been a Nightmare Detective?" Slim asked, smirking as Uko took a big swig.

"How did you know?"

"Detectives are easy to spot. Especially in a place like this."

"Since the summer," Uko replied. "So a couple months now."

"What's your name?"

"Uko."

"Cool," Slim said before taking a big gulp of his own. He fell silent for a few awkward moments.

"So what's your nightmare about?" Uko asked.

Slim turned to Uko and reached into his pocket. He pulled out a small white cell phone and placed it on the bar between them.

"This little thing here," he said while pointing to it.

"The phone?"

"Yeah." Slim picked it up and examined it as if for the first time. "Every night I dream about being here at this bar by myself. I have a few drinks, I watch a few singers, I chat with a couple people—normal stuff. Then this phone rings."

Slim stopped speaking. Uko patiently waited for him to continue, but he didn't. A sinking feeling crept in.

"Then what?" he asked.

Slim put down the phone and wiped his eye. He looked at his glass for a moment before he spoke again.

"Then I answer it and hear the worst news I could possibly receive. There's a voice on the other end telling me that my entire family just died. My wife. My daughter. My little boy." His voice caught for a moment. "Plane crash on their way back from a family trip."

Uko stared at Slim in shocked silence. This was much more than he expected.

"Everyone I've cared for and loved. Just like that." He finished his drink with another big gulp and waved the bartender over. She immediately replaced it with another full glass. "You wanna know why I'm not with them?"

Uko looked at his drink.

"Because I'd rather be here."

Uko looked around in silence. Once again, the dozens of people in shadows throughout the busy room stopped what they were doing to return his glance as he looked. He quickly turned back to Slim.

"What if you don't answer it?" he asked.

Slim nodded his head. "I thought of that. But it just keeps ringing. I gotta answer." He picked the phone up again and held it to the light to get a better look at it. "Every night I gotta answer. Every night it hurts just the same."

Uko felt overmatched. Since becoming a Detective, he'd only helped kids around his age. This was his first adult and he wasn't sure why this was his assignment. Even though it was daunting, he was determined to pass the test.

"I'll answer it then," Uko said quietly. Slim gave him a puzzled look. "Maybe that will change things."

"You know what? I've never thought of that. Doubt that changes anything, though."

As soon as Slim finished the question, the phone rang loudly—much louder than expected. The entire room fell silent instantly as every pair of eyes rested on Uko and Slim. Uko held his breath.

"What should we do?" Slim asked. The ring was getting louder by the moment. Uko heard the sound of chairs screeching against the floor as people in the room began standing to get a better look at them. He reached out and took it from Slim. He couldn't tell whether the vibration he felt was from the phone or his own hands quivering under pressure. He tapped the answer button, placed it to his ear, and heard silence on the other end.

"Hello?" he said tentatively.

"Who is this?" came a confused voice. Uko eyed Slim for reassurance. He was expressionless as the crowd pressed in on all sides.

"This is Uko," he finally said.

There was a pause. "Okay. Is Charles there?"

Slim gave no direction, so Uko whispered back, "Um, he just walked away for a second." It was the first thing that came to him.

"Tell him that we're waiting at the airport. He's late, and the kids are tired. This is Vicky, by the way," the voice added before hanging up.

Uko closed the flip phone and handed it back to Slim. "Vicky said they're waiting for you at the airport. Is that them?"

Slim stared at Uko in silence for a few tense seconds. "Oh my God," Slim said softly. "That worked, 'lil man!" The crowd that hovered around them broke out into loud applause. They clapped Uko on the back as they returned to their seats. Uko swelled with a mixture of pride and relief.

"I can't believe you did it," Slim said, laughing. "I owe you." He stood up and waved for the bartender's attention again.

"No, it's fine. That's my job," Uko said bashfully.

"No, no, I insist," Slim interrupted. He rummaged around in his pockets. "I know you're young, but I feel like I need to get you a drink."

"No, I'm fine, really," Uko said. He stood up to walk out. Slim placed his hand on his chest and stopped him.

"I know exactly what I can give you. Have a seat." When Uko sat back down, Slim pulled out a small blue box emblazoned with elaborate gold patterns. He cradled it as if it were a secret and leaned in close before allowing him to see it clearly. The gold shimmered so vividly it seemed to dance. "Do you know what this is?"

Uko shook his head. Slim checked for eavesdroppers. When he was satisfied that there weren't any, he leaned in closer and practically whispered in Uko's ear. "This is the Watch of Nana. This box holds the time of Pangea in its entirety. Have you ever been given a gift in Pangea?" Slim asked.

"No."

"Well, this is one hell of a first. You won't ever get something as special as this again, mark my words," Slim said, holding the box out to Uko. "You're smart, kid. You deserve it." Uko took it, surprised at how heavy the tiny object felt in his hands.

"That heaviness you feel is the weight of this world. There's a lot of responsibility in that box."

"What does it do?" Uko asked, caressing the gold patterns. He was awed by its beauty.

"It is the keeper of all time in Pangea. Whoever owns it can stop time throughout all of this land by opening it," Slim said. "If you opened it now, we would all freeze in time along with everyone else dreaming around the world. All things would pause. All things except for you. You would get free rein in a world frozen in place."

Uko was stunned. "Why would someone want to do that?"

Slim stood up and threw on the coat hung on his chair. "Because you would eventually need to close it again." When his coat was on, he bent down and whispered in Uko's ear again. "Whoever you're touching when you close the box gets pulled into it. Their entire essence gets locked away in that tiny box."

"Forever?" Uko asked.

"Yes sir," Slim said with a smile as he stepped back. "That's the only way to close it. That weight is from everyone who has been put into the box before it made its way to your little hands."

Uko's hands sagged under its weight. He held it out. "I don't want to put anyone in this."

"Are you sure?" Slim asked. He pushed the box back toward Uko. "Think about it. You're a Nightmare Detective. I'm sure you can think of at least one person that Pangea would be better without."

Uko's mind danced around. "I'm serious, I'm not that kind of guy. I couldn't lock someone away forever. That's evil."

Slim laughed loudly. Half of the room turned their attention back to him. "Nothing is that simple, kid. You can use it for evil, sure. But you can also use it for good. It depends on your intentions." Slim sat back down. "That box is filled with the essence of both good and bad people. Some people before you have used it to settle grudges. But others have used it to make Pangea a better place. If you rid this place of someone who's actually evil, then is that wrong?"

Uko considered Slim's words. He thought about how it could apply to him and tried to see how he could make Pangea a better place by using it. Suddenly, his separate and random thoughts landed on a single, clear image in his mind. "Chief," he whispered to himself.

Slim looked at him silently. Uko tried to read Slim's face to see if he had heard Chief's name slip out of his mouth. Slim's face told no tales.

"The owner of Nana's Watch knows best. It'll be at your DreamHub every night. Take it whenever you think you'll need it. You don't have to carry it around with you all the time. But one night, it'll come in handy and you'll do the right thing because of it. Then we'll be even," Slim said. He walked a few steps toward the door before turning back. "Thanks again for all your help."

"You're welcome," Uko said softly as Slim left. Uko stuffed the box in his pocket.

"Chief," he said to himself again. The hairs on his body stood tall at the thought. "I'm gonna be the Detective who gets rid of Chief."

CHAPTER 5

Ongoing Investigation

THE NEXT DAY AT SCHOOL, Uko's mind was preoccupied with thoughts of Pangea, Slim, and Nana's Watch.

"Just gotta find him, that's all," Uko said to himself as he tossed his math textbook on top of the unruly mess in his locker. "Shouldn't be too hard."

He picked up his US history book and placed it on the floor next to him before diving back into the pile. "I'll just hold a sign over my head," Uko added, chuckling. After a few more minutes of searching, he finally found the workbook he needed for art class. He held it up in triumph before going back to his thoughts. "I wonder if he'd see it coming."

He took one step back and closed the locker door, spotting a figure out of the corner of his eye. A person less than one foot away was leaning against the locker next to his. Brandon's face was so close to Uko that it took a second for his eyes to register his presence.

"What's up?" Brandon said.

Uko gasped, then winced as if he were protecting himself from an incoming dodgeball. His heart skipping two or three beats, Uko picked up the art workbook that he'd dropped in surprise. "What's wrong with you? You play too much?"

Brandon smothered his laugh with a hand. "Wow. I can't believe that worked."

"Shut up," Uko replied, walking away.

Brandon followed. "Did you think about my plan? Are you in on solving this thing with me or what?"

"Oh, my bad. I forgot about that."

"You forgot? How could you forget?" Brandon asked as the homeroom bell rang. "You too busy or something?"

"Nah, he's not busy," Manny said as he walked up to Brandon and Uko. "Don't let him try and fool you."

"So, do you want in or no?" Brandon asked the boys. "'Cause I'm gonna do it either way."

"You think we can do it?" Uko asked Manny.

"Yeah, we got it," Manny replied.

"Cool. Then we're in," Uko said. "What's the plan?"

"Good. Y'all gonna like this," Brandon said, rushing to homeroom. "I'll meet you here after school and we'll go over what to do next."

"You really think we're gonna find some crazy conspiracy with Ms. Kowalski?" Uko asked Manny.

"Probably not, but it'll give us something to do," Manny replied. "Let's worry about getting to homeroom on time before we get written up."

"What are you starting with today?" Manny asked Uko.

"Mr. Kittles—Social Studies."

"You're lucky, he's the cool teacher," Manny whined. "I got English with Ms. Tan first. I heard she's mad boring."

"Glad I have Ms. Phelps for English then. Don't forget to meet me and Brandon at my locker. I'm not gonna try to crack this case by myself."

"Sure," Manny said. "See you later."

The boys bumped fists and went their separate ways. Uko sighed as he entered the classroom and saw that most of the desks in the middle and back were already filled. He reluctantly slid into a desk front and center as the teacher wrote on the board. The class was buzzing with students, all of whom seemed to know each other by their chatting and giggling. The feeling of isolation reminded him of what made the blog investigation so intriguing. People stick with who they already know, so he'd be better off staying low-key and anonymous instead of trying to insert himself into cliques. When the bell for class rang, the teacher turned back around.

"Good morning, everyone!" he shouted excitedly. "My name is Mr. Kittles and this is US History. You may have heard that I'm the coolest teacher in this school." He paused. "That is correct."

The class laughed.

"But don't be fooled," Mr. Kittles continued. "You will do some real work in this class, and I expect you to hold your own. I'm gonna treat you all like growing kids who will be young adults soon. Don't make me have to treat you differently. Make sense?"

"Yes," the class said in unison.

"We'll be covering as much as we can—from the Native Americans and the first pilgrims, to the World Wars, to Kim Kardashian and today," Mr. Kittles said with a smile. His hair was twisted into waist-length locs that he kept in a loose ponytail. As he spoke, he tucked a stray loc behind his ear. "I know today is usually the day you coast and just find out about the plans for the year, but I don't want to do that. I like to put you guys on the spot."

A hushed murmur went through the group of students. Uko looked around to see if other people knew what was coming but couldn't get any clues.

"Now I have your attention, huh? Good. I'm going to pick two students for a head-to-head quiz on history in front of the class. Winner gets a check by their name in my notebook." He held up a small composition notebook. "The person with the most checks each month gets a prize."

"What's the prize?" someone behind Uko asked.

"It's a surprise," Mr. Kittles answered. "It changes each month. But you'll like it, I promise. Who's up for it?" No one raised their hands. Mr. Kittles waited a few moments while scanning the room. "Don't make me choose people," he continued, but still no one responded. "Okay. When I call you, walk up to the front of the class with me."

Uko tried to look forward in a way that wouldn't draw attention to himself. Mr. Kittles pointed at him before excitedly clapping his hands. "The good ol' look away without looking away. Well done. You'll be my first choice! What's your name?"

Uko dropped his head in defeat. "Uko."

"Say it again?" Mr. Kittles asked while stepping closer. A few students chuckled. "Class, settle down."

"It's Uko."

"Uko?

"Yes."

"Is that Nigerian?" Mr. Kittles asked.

"Yeah," Uko replied, eyebrows raised.

"I knew it. My roommate in college was named Uko, and he was Nigerian." He looked back around the class. "Who wants to go against Uko?"

Uko scanned the faces of the rest of the students as he joined Mr. Kittles in front of the class. He only recognized two people in the class of twenty. When he got to the front, a hand slowly rose from the back of the room.

"I'll go." A tall boy in a dark blue hoodie stood up, ignoring the stares from the rest of the class. He held his head high and poked out his chest as he confidently strutted to the front. Two boys stuck out their hands for high-fives as he passed. To Uko, he looked old enough to be a senior in high school.

"And what's your name, young man?" Mr. Kittles asked as the boy reached the front.

"Cory," he replied. "Cory Simms. Everybody calls me Simms."

"Simms? Okay, great. Class, we have Simms versus Uko. I'm going to ask them a series of questions to see what they know about American history. They get five seconds to answer. No one can help them." He reached into his pocket, pulled out a bright red buzzer from the game Taboo, and handed it to a girl sitting in the front row. He bent over and asked the girl for her name. She shyly whispered back. "If they get it wrong, then Kiarah here will give them the buzz. Let me hear that buzz, Kiarah."

Kiarah pressed down on the large red button and it buzzed loudly. The class broke out in laughter. "Perfect. Now let's get started. Gentlemen, shake hands."

Uko held his hand out to Simms. He glanced down at it, smirked, then looked back toward the class. A loud "ooooh" filled the room.

"All right, just for that, Simms will get the first question. Let's give him a hard one," Mr. Kittles said as he shuffled through his index cards. "In the mid-1800s, Native Americans were forced to relocate to designated reserves in the West. They had to march to these destinations with militia. What were these forced relocations called?"

"The Trail of Tears!" Simms shouted just seconds after Mr. Kittles finished. He held his chest out again, smirking at Uko.

"Correct!" Mr. Kittles cried out. The class clapped their approval.

"Wow, tried to stump you with a tricky one but you were ready," Mr. Kittles said. "Good job. Okay, it's Uko's turn. Uko, the United States began as thirteen colonies which ended up being states on the East Coast. Name three of them."

Uko's mind went blank as Mr. Kittles finished the question. He panicked for a split second before the names rushed back to him. "New York, New Jersey, and, um, Delaware."

"Correct!" The class did not clap as enthusiastically for Uko as they did for Simms.

"Simms, your turn. Which artist has the most sold albums ever among US musicians?"

Simms squinted his eyes and looked to the ground. "Uh...” The class seemed to lean forward. "Michael Jackson." He looked over at Kiarah and her buzzer. She looked down at her cheatsheet, looked back up, and pressed the button with all her might. A loud buzz and the sound of laughter broke the silence.

"Nope!" Mr. Kittles said. "He's number two on the list. Uko, you can take his points if you know the answer."

Uko had thought it was Michael Jackson too, so he guessed the name of someone he heard was also popular back in the day. "Elvis?" he asked.

"Correct!" Mr. Kittles shouted. Uko reflexively threw his hands in the air. Simms stared daggers at him.

"Okay, we're going to go for the best out of three. If Uko gets this right, he wins. If Simms gets it right, we move to sudden death. I'll make it interesting and start with Simms again," Mr. Kittles said. He playfully strode between the students, drawing out the tension. "Simms, the 'I Have a Dream' speech delivered by Dr. Martin Luther King is considered one of the greatest speeches of all time. In what year did he deliver that speech?"

Simms' eyes darted to the ground. Uko didn't know the answer himself and was hoping Simms was in the same boat. "1960," Simms said before pausing. The class leaned forward. Mr. Kittles stopped pacing and waited. "No, wait, 1963."

"Is that your final answer?" Mr. Kittles asked.

"Yeah."

"You sure you don't want to change it?"

"I'm sure. 1963."

"That is correct!" Mr. Kittles yelled as the class broke out into applause. Uko felt the weight of Simms' glare. This time, he had a maniacal grin on his face.

"All right, so we're in Sudden Death. Whoever gets this right is the winner. They get bragging rights from day one. Who will it be, class?" Mr. Kittles asked. The class yelled out "Simms" in near perfect unison. Simms waved his arms like a conductor in front of an orchestra. His large build now seemed more imposing than ever.

"Gentlemen," Mr. Kittles said. He waited until the din of noise in the room quieted before he continued. "In September 2000, television network MTV premiered one of the most important documentary shows of all time. A show that would bring you into the homes of your favorite celebrities. What is the name of this—"

"Cribs! MTV Cribs!" Uko blurted out before Mr. Kittles could finish.

"What?!" Simms yelled at Uko. "You gotta wait until he finishes the question." The crowd joined in with loud complaints.

Mr. Kittles chuckled to himself and looked around. Uko looked at Mr. Kittles for clarification. Feeling guilty, he waited for Mr. Kittles to declare Simms today's winner.

"I never said you have to wait for the full question, Simms." Both the rowdy class and Simms erupted in anger at this. Mr. Kittles spent several minutes quieting everyone down. When the class was quiet enough, Uko began asking

Mr. Kittles if they could just do another question, but Mr. Kittles would not let him finish.

"It's over, fellas. Uko won. Simms, you lost."

"Are you kidding? He cheated!" Simms said aggressively. Uko looked at him with a blank face, but internally he wanted nothing more than to have this entire thing end as soon as possible. He didn't want to get on the bad side of a classmate so early.

Mr. Kittles told the boys to go back to their seats as he quieted the classroom. As Simms walked by Uko, he purposefully nudged him with his shoulder and whispered something under his breath. They sat down and Mr. Kittles continued with his first lesson. When the bell rang and everyone bolted out of the room, Mr. Kittles called Uko over to his desk. He waited until every student left before beginning his conversation.

"Sorry that I didn't get your name the first time you said it. I know it's annoying to have teachers repeat it again and again," he said.

"That's fine," Uko replied.

"How do you like the class so far?" Mr. Kittles asked. "Do you think you'll learn a lot?"

"I like it. I think I'll do well, Mr. Kittles," Uko responded.

"You can call me Mr. K. That's what everyone calls me."

"Okay," Uko replied before jumping into the question that was on his mind. "Why didn't you just let me and Simms do a different question? Didn't you see how upset he was?"

"Yeah, I saw. He'll be all right," Mr. Kittles said as he began cleaning up stray papers around his desk. "Everything's not always fair. Sometimes you gotta use any advantage you have to win."

"Like cheat?"

"You didn't cheat. You used a loophole. That's different," Mr. K said as he tossed the papers in the garbage. "Now the class will pay better attention to the rules of the game. Enjoy your day, Uko."

"Thanks. You too," Uko said as he turned and walked out of the class. He was happy that he'd won the competition with Simms, but wished he wasn't a part of life lessons along the way.

The rest of the school day passed without incident. He met his new teachers and learned how things would be different now that he was in middle school. "This isn't like elementary school! You're big boys and girls now," was the thing every teacher said in some form. It left him somewhere between wishing he was still among the oldest kids in his elementary school and being excited to start a new journey. At any given point of the day, his feelings would swing from one extreme to the other. At least he had Manny to go through it with him.

"You ready to dig into conspiracies with Brandon?" Manny asked as he approached Uko's locker at the end of the last class. "How was your first day?"

"It was all right," Uko casually responded. He put his things away, grabbed his coat, and walked with Manny to the front of the school. They looked around for Brandon but couldn't find him. "Did he tell you where we should meet him after school?"

"No," Manny replied as he continued looking around.

After looking for a few more moments, the two boys both settled on watching the other students pour out of the building. They stared as the kids laughed and began walking home in groups of four or five. Every few minutes, a car would pull up and a kid would scurry into the back as if they did not want to be seen. Uko knew that if he were getting picked up in front of school, he would feel the same way. As he stood there staring with Manny, Uko flinched as someone dropped a heavy hand on his right shoulder. Brandon stood behind Manny and Uko with his arms around each boy. He found this especially funny.

"Caught y'all sleepin'," Brandon said. "You're gonna have to be more vigilant if you wanna be a part of my investigation."

"Stop doing that," Uko said, thoroughly annoyed.

This only made Brandon laugh more. "Okay, I'll take it easy on you. I'll use my powers for good and turn you into spies like James Bond."

"Whatever, Brandon," Manny said. "Just tell us what your plan is. What's the super-secret mystery?"

Brandon peeled away from Manny and Uko and looked around as if he thought they might be overheard. When he seemed satisfied that no one was eavesdropping, he turned back to the boys and lowered his voice.

"Never talk about what we're doing out in the open and never talk about it with anyone else, because you can get us all in serious trouble," Brandon said. "From now on, we only use codenames for what we're doing and for each other. You get me? We use those names and those names only from now on."

"What are they?" Uko asked.

"This is Operation Mongoose. Uko, your codename is Anansi. Manny, you're Duende. And I'm John Henry."

Uko and Manny looked at each other with smirks. This all seemed silly. Manny rolled his eyes. "Are you serious?"

"Dead serious. We've been following this thing since last year," Brandon said, walking closer. "The school knows someone's on to them. Three of us have gotten detentions because of this already. This is not a game."

CHAPTER 6

Operation Mongoose

I guess this is serious, Uko thought.

"What's this all about?" Uko asked.

"Where do you guys live?" Brandon replied.

"By Branch Brook," Manny said.

"All right, cool. I'm up that way so we can walk and talk," Brandon said. "I'll start from the beginning. Try and keep up, kids."

They started their trek back home. They crossed the busy street in front of the school and turned onto Park Avenue on their way back home. Brandon walked silently as they passed stray students while they were still close to the building. As they got farther away and ended up by themselves, he began his rundown.

"I don't run Last Word. I just write on it from time to time. Everyone uses codenames that we sign our posts with. Like I said before, mine is John Henry. When we come up with a story, we all send it in and see what the editor chooses. Sometimes you might get an email back with notes on changing the story."

"What's the editor's codename?" Manny asked.

"Nellie S," Brandon said. "No idea who that is in the school. Just know that she's a girl."

"Got it," Uko said as they stopped at a crosswalk while cars flew by. "What's this story about?"

"Mongoose."

"Right, what's Operation Mongoose about?" Uko clarified.

"Why do you wanna do this?" Brandon asked.

"I think it's cool. I like to write," he said as he searched his mind for more answers. "We joined Coding Club to meet people, and then we met you and heard about all the blog and everything. This sounds way more interesting."

Brandon looked unimpressed. He turned to Manny. "You?"

"Same as him."

Brandon looked even more unimpressed and rolled his eyes. "This isn't something to just pass the time."

"I know," both Manny and Uko said.

"We wanna be a part of something dope instead of just dying of boredom in class then going home every day. This is definitely something different. And since we can do this all kinda undercover, we don't have to put ourselves out there and get in trouble for anything crazy, right?" Uko added.

"If we do this right, no one is gonna know you were involved. Just the aliases," Brandon replied. "I wanna take over for Nellie someday and this is my shot. I nail this and it's a wrap. I'm definitely running Last Word next year," Brandon added. "But I need help, so here we are."

"Did you ask the other kids in Coding Club?" Uko asked.

"Nah, I think they're in on it," Brandon replied.

"What exactly is it?" Manny asked. "You haven't said that yet."

Brandon squinted at the two of them. "I'm gonna give you what you need to get started. If you're good at finding info, then I'll give you more. That's how we'll do this for now."

"All right, man," Uko said while shaking his head. "Mad dramatic for no reason."

Brandon ignored him and glanced around one last time before continuing. "Ms. Kowalski has been the mean old lady who runs the computer department for years. She never does more than required. I swear she hates her job. You ask her a question during class, she makes it seem like you're begging her for money or something. Then last year out of nowhere, she starts a Coding Club that would make her stay after school twice a week."

The boys huddled close to Brandon as he spoke. Now that he was giving them real information, it seemed the city noise of Newark was at its highest. They squeezed past other kids as they exited their schools and spilled into the street. More than once they had to walk in single file to slide past crowded bus stops with commuters covering the entire sidewalk. School dismissal was organized chaos throughout the city.

"It's strange enough that Ms. Kowalski of all people would start a club. But then I started hearing about people trying to join and being turned away. I also noticed that it was never advertised like the other clubs were. It was if you had to already know it existed to even try and join, and even then you might not get in," Brandon continued. "After a while, kids were asking to join just to see if they could make it. She only let a few random kids in for a while until the school made her let more people join. That's how I got in."

"What happened when the other kids joined?" Manny asked.

"Pretty much nothing," Brandon replied. "She made us watch the same dumb playlist of 'Intro to Making Video Games' videos on YouTube, didn't teach us anything, and was really mean when people asked questions. Eventually people stopped showing up."

Uko scratched his eyebrow. "Why do you think she's doing that?"

"I'm not sure. She started this club for a reason, and it's not to teach coding or make games because I haven't done any of that yet. I walk to the back and she never checks in on me. She spends all her time with those kids up front who were there when you two came in," Brandon answered.

Manny threw up his arms. "Why don't you just ask what they're doing?"

"You don't think I ever asked? Of course I did. They don't say anything, and Ms. Kowalski changes the subject by asking me if I've watched all the stupid intro videos. There's like a hundred of them," Brandon said. He pointed to a pizzeria across the street from where they were walking. "You guys ever get a slice from there? It's good."

"Nah," Uko and Manny said in unison. "Have you learned anything about what she's doing yet?" Uko added.

"The only thing I'm learning is how to make Pac-Man."

"So what do you want us to do?" Manny asked. Uko had the same thought. If Brandon couldn't figure it out, what were they supposed to add? This mission to get to the bottom of things sounded less promising than he hoped.

The group stopped at the end of the street as Brandon pointed up a new block. "I'm up this way," he said. "What we're gonna do is get to know those kids in the front of the class. I don't think they're all a part of the secret. Maybe between the three of us, we can get close enough to the right one to figure something out."

"What if all of this is just a waste of time?" Manny said. "You're not even sure what you're looking for."

"I'm sorry, do you have something better to do?" Brandon shot back. "You just told me that you're trying to meet people, and you're bored. This is your best chance at solving both of those problems. Besides, even if we don't find anything really interesting, you can at least make your debuts on Last Word as Anansi and Duende. Eventually you can meet some of the other writers on the blog. I've never met Nellie, but I can introduce you to some of the other people if you prove you're cool."

Even though Uko watched Manny roll his eyes, he liked the idea. There probably wasn't anything special going on, but he'd at least have some excitement in a new school. There was just one thing that worried him. "Why did the other kids get detentions?"

"That's a good question, Anansi," Brandon said, walking backwards up the block. "That's a real good question. You're a natural." Brandon smiled, turned around and dashed toward his house. He yelled out, "See you tomorrow!" over his shoulder as he got farther away. Manny and Uko shared a look.

"This is all your fault," Manny said. "John Henry is your fault."

Uko laughed. "I don't see a problem. We're Detectives!"

"Don't you start with that, Uko!"

They walked the rest of the way back home in relative silence, taking in the city's daily sights and sounds as they unwound from a long day of school. Uko watched as cars honked while weaving through traffic. The boys nodded at people sitting on their front porches and stoops. They tugged on their bookbag straps and ambled along as the city around them buzzed with its familiar after-school chorus of activity.

"All right, I'll see you tomorrow," Manny said to Uko as they approached his house.

"Tell Carlos I said what's up."

"He said we gotta do something different this weekend. Since it's gonna be cold soon, we gotta take advantage of the weather," Manny said.

"All right, cool." His mind was already on thoughts of ending his day and getting back to Pangea. They dapped and parted ways. Uko walked to his door and waited while Manny walked past two more houses and climbed the steps to his door.

That evening, after homework was done, dinner was eaten, and the house was settling in for bed, Uko could freely think about the Watch of Nana and his plan to get rid of Chief. *Pangea's gonna be a better place*, he thought while brushing his teeth. *I'll be a hero, the Coyotes will stop terrorizing people, and everyone will be happy.* All he had to do was find Chief. That was the hard part.

As Uko lay down, he turned to face his dresser and looked at Kanju one last time before he fell asleep. He imagined the stuffed animal giving him a subtle nod of acknowledgement before his eyes drifted closed, and he returned to his second home.

Uko found himself standing alone in the quiet meadow he knew so well. He raised his hands high over his head and leaned back in an exaggerated stretch. "Well, well, well. We meet again," he said to himself. The thick trees and the imposing shadows the surrounding forest cast were no longer things he feared. They signaled the beginning of his Silk Road. They represented new clients, new adventures, new skills. He walked to them with his arms open wide, feeling blessed to tread that dark path. It was a privilege to stand in front of his DreamHub and select his next destination. It was his calling.

When his breezy stroll got Uko to the base of the path, he immediately began searching for the box that he had been given in last night's dream—the key to ending the struggle with Chief. After a few moments of casually glancing around, the fear of being played started to creep in. He wondered if Slim had pulled a nasty trick on him, and he walked around the thick tree trunks in a deep squat as he searched with his hands. The anxiety only grew as he frantically cleared away brush, twigs and rocks. He whirled around another tree in frustration, stubbing his toe on what felt like a heavy root. Catching the faint shimmer of something metallic buried under dirt, he reached down and pulled out the ornate box he was handed last night—The Watch of Nana. It looked even more splendid than he remembered. He held it up to his eyes and felt its surprising weight. A small smile crept across his face. This was it. He tucked it into his pocket and began his walk down the path. He was back on his mission.

When the twists and turns in the dark led Uko to his beloved DreamHub, he breathed deeply as the familiar fog rolled down from the sky. It spilled over his feet and seemed to mix freely with the quiet air of the forest. The deep purples and silver highlights shimmered and tinted the images that presented themselves in the midst. He took in the massive curtain of moving figures that danced before him. He turned to what looked like a group of friends laughing together. He glanced down by his knees and saw a girl walking among various animals of different sizes. Even though trial and error had made him better at the process, it was still difficult for Uko to decipher the various things he saw

in the fog. They moved quickly, were always somewhat vague, and were usually replaced by something else after a few moments.

Where can I find Chief? Uko said to himself. *Where in the world can he be?*

Just then, Uko saw a shift in the fog to the right of him. The once thick stream broke apart. Uko walked over to it as it pulled back together and slowly revealed an image of people standing perfectly still. It stood out considering all of the other images in a DreamHub were constantly in motion. He stepped back to see how much of the fog was a part of this frozen frame and noticed something that looked like a large dog near their feet. It was the only thing moving as it paced slowly back and forth among the frozen group of people.

"What is that?" he asked aloud before a thought crossed his mind. *Is that a coyote?* As he said it, the animal in the frame turned toward Uko, ears perked as if it had heard him. Uko stumbled back, startled. After a few seconds of waiting for something to happen and seeing that it wouldn't, Uko shakily stuck his hand out toward the image. The silver and purples enveloped his fingers and then his hand and then his arm. The rest of the fog retreated from around him and wrapped itself around his body. He wasn't sure where he was headed next but hoped that he'd like the destination.

CHAPTER 7

King of Pangea

BANG!

The familiar flash of white light from jumping into Pangea was always so powerful it felt like an explosion. He blinked repeatedly as his surroundings came into focus. Ahead of him was a row of blue lockers. To his right and left, he saw large cinder blocks painted in bright colors and covered in children's artwork. He immediately recognized that he was in a school hallway. He might not know which school he stood in, but the "Always Do Your Best" wall posters had been standard issue in every school he'd ever attended.

As normally happened when jumping into dreams, there was a delay before the sound of his surroundings came to him. There was a full-on party going on, a fact that became more and more apparent as the volume slowly turned up. People cheered as laughter mixed in with the thumping of music. Uko pressed his back against the wall at the end of the hall and peered around the corner, leery.

Adults in formal tuxedos and colorful dresses streamed in and out of a room, holding glasses in their hands and dancing. As he surveyed the scene, he recognized the upbeat Nigerian music that his mom played Saturday mornings when it was time to clean the house. He could hear someone on a microphone instruct everyone to get on the dance floor. The couples outside the room rushed back in as the voice spoke. When the hall was clear, Uko walked around the corner and approached the door to the party. He looked down and saw himself in a black tuxedo, perfect for the occasion.

"Shower money on the lovely couple!" the microphone voice boomed as Uko reached the now closed door.

When he opened the door, the sounds of music and celebration flooded out into the hall. What had once been a school gymnasium was transformed into a reception hall. Tables with elaborate centerpieces surrounded a crowded dance floor. In the center, Uko saw the backs of a bride and groom as they held hands and danced enthusiastically. Around them was a circle of onlookers who tossed so much money into the air it looked like confetti. As the bills floated down onto the couple like falling leaves, little girls with bags picked up what fell to the ground. *It's a Nigerian wedding*, Uko thought to himself as he walked toward the dancing bride and groom. Just as he finally relaxed and began thinking about how nice this all looked, there was a loud slam behind him, followed by a frightening scream.

He turned around to see what looked like a dark gray dog charge into the room as the crowd rushed toward the opposite wall. The sight paralyzed him. Right behind the dog, a small group of men and women, all dressed in crimson red tuxedos, confidently strode into the room. They stood and stared at Uko as the dog sat on its hind legs and let out a loud howl. Before Uko could register what was happening, another figure entered the room. From the flowing crimson and blue dashiki, the dark glasses, and cane, Uko immediately knew that he was face to face with Chief again.

The crowd continued to scream as they ran to the other side of the room and left Uko stranded in the middle. Chief walked slowly towards Uko as a mischievous smile appeared on his lips.

Even though Uko had hoped to find Chief, the actual sight of him was more terrifying than what he was prepared for.

"Did you miss me?" Chief asked before bellowing a howl of his own. The group in red tuxedos returned his call with their own howls. They began advancing toward Uko and the crowd behind him.

He sped backwards, his hands clenched in tight fists. He was overwhelmed but knew that his window to act was closing. He reached into the pocket of his tuxedo in search of Nana's Box. His hands brushed against the cold metal, and he tried to yank it out. Instead, he tripped on his backpedaling feet and stumbled to the ground. His fear and effort to pull the box so quickly from his pocket flung it clear across the room. His eyes followed the box as it slid toward the wedding guests, pressing themselves against the wall.

"No!"

"Uh-oh," Chief mockingly called out. "Did you drop something, my friend?" The well-dressed Coyotes that flanked Chief laughed as they closed in.

Uko looked at the person closest to the box and made eye contact with him. It was the groom. He stood by his bride as the box skidded to his feet. Uko stumbled to his knees and breathlessly pointed to it.

"Throw that to me. Quickly!"

The groom bent down quickly and scooped up the box. When he did, he stared at Uko and shook it. *This?* he seemed to ask.

"Yes," Uko replied. "Throw it!" He prayed that the man had good aim. At the same time, he noticed something vaguely familiar about him.

"Here you go, 'lil man," the groom said before tossing the box to Uko.

It felt like time slowed down as the box flew through the air. It took the last inch of his fingertips to keep the box from sailing over his head. When he finally had it in his grasp, Uko whirled onto his back to see how close the Coyotes were. He saw them less than a foot away, hands outstretched as he fumbled the box open, held his breath, and shut his eyes. Every muscle in his body contracted in silent prayer that this actually worked. Otherwise, he was screwed.

The room that was once filled with hectic noise was now completely silent. All he could hear was his labored breathing. He slowly opened one eye to see the Coyotes frozen above him. He opened his other eye and scanned the room. The wedding guests were against the wall mid-scream. He sat up. Chief was still as stone, that same smile across his face. He could hardly believe his eyes.

"Oh my God," Uko said to himself. "It worked!" He jumped up and down in triumph. Laughing, he turned back toward the wedding party. The sight of so many people frozen in place had an eerie effect.

Uko thought about the instructions he had been given with the box. The words of Slim came to him as he circled the Coyotes who had been moments away from seizing him.

Uko could see Slim's face as his mind's eye recalled his words. "It's the keeper of all time in Pangea," he said when describing the box. "Open it and all things would pause. All things except for you. You would get free rein in a world frozen in place."

Uko beamed at the sight of those words now in action. Now, all he had to do was touch Chief while he closed the box and he would be trapped inside it. Even though he did not move, Chief was still incredibly imposing. Up close, Uko could see every tear in his clothing, the scar that stretched across his face, the dark glasses. This close, Chief's smell nearly overwhelmed Uko. The concoction of musty, moldy clothing and intense body odor wafted from him. Uko's heart beat rapidly as he approached him, but he ignored the smell as he reached out to touch the cause of so much pain in his beloved Pangea.

"Here we go," Uko said as he reached out for Chief. "Goodbye."

"Uko!" a voice screamed. The suddenness of it brought on an explosion of adrenaline, and he jerked his head in its direction. To his horror, he saw the groom striding toward him with his arms outstretched. "You remember me?"

As Uko's eyes settled on the man's face, his mind finally made the connection. There was a reason he looked so familiar.

"Slim?" Uko said. He finally recognized the face of the man who'd given him this magical gift. The second the words left his lips, Uko let out a scream. There was a sharp, piercing sensation under his arm.

"ARGH!" Uko yelled in pain. It felt like being shocked with electricity. Stunned, he slowly turned back toward Chief and was baffled with what he saw. Instead of being an arm's length away from Uko, Chief was so close that Uko could feel Chief's breath as he spoke.

"Surprise, surprise," Chief whispered. Uko could now feel his other arm being held by Chief while the sharp pain grew worse. He slowly pulled a long blade out of Uko's ribcage. The pain intensified, and Uko's vision became blurry.

"You..." Uko said groggily, "you stabbed me." Things were going dim, but he was close enough to Chief to see his lips curl into another smile. He could hear Slim begin to laugh.

"They never said these Detectives were bright," Chief said as he gently pushed Uko down. Pain exploded in his side as he hit the ground. He tried to remind himself that this was a dream, but it certainly didn't feel that way.

"Don't trust everyone you meet, 'lil man," Uko heard as he grabbed his now bleeding wound and curled in on himself.

"I was worried it wouldn't be worth canceling all of my appointments to come here tonight," Chief said. "It takes a lot to pull me away from torturing a family."

Uko briefly looked up to see Slim and Chief standing over him. Their blurred faces became increasingly dimmer and dimmer. Chief kneeled over him and placed his hand on Uko's chest.

"Long live the King of Pangea."

◆ ◆ ◆

Uko's senses slowly came back to him one by one. His hearing returned first. Moans of pain erupted from the darkness around him. Next came touch. His skin and the clothes he wore were damp. He could feel the prickle of rocks under his back where he lay. Taste and smell reappeared in tandem. The air was so thick with sooty ash that he could practically chew it. Finally, his vision returned. He could see a starry sky above him; he was surrounded by walls of dirt. Sitting up, he touched the place where Chief's blade had pierced him. There was no pain or wound.

As he stood up, Uko felt the dirt wall pressing in on him. Once fully standing, it was clear he was actually in a hole. With some worried effort, he placed his hands on the cool ground and pulled himself out.

"Where the heck am I?"

He was shocked to find that the hole he had just emerged from was similar to the dozens of craters that pockmarked the ground as far as he could see. Now that he was out of his own hole, the sound of the moans loudened. He peeked in the nearest one and recoiled at the sight of a girl staring back at him.

The land was so covered in holes that there were only slivers of flat land between them. As Uko stood on his toes and anxiously looked into some of the nearby pits, he quickly realized that each was inhabited. His heart stampeded in his chest as the realization set in. He didn't know where he should go or where he currently was, but he was overcome with the feeling that it wouldn't be wise to remain here. He scanned the horizon and noticed a flat area covered in grass a few hundred feet to his left. He immediately began weaving between the craters, doing his best to not look into them. The chorus of wails made moving quickly even more difficult. From time to time, his footing would slip, and he'd feel himself spill into one of the holes. The panic would be enough to snap him to attention and pull his foot back to flat ground.

At one point, someone grabbed his shoe and jerked it down. Flying chunks of dirt and the nighttime darkness made it impossible to see who grabbed him, so he kicked relentlessly in the general direction, sending his sneaker sliding off into the hole. He pulled his foot back as he stood and began running toward the grass as fast as he could, staring pointedly at the ground ahead of him as he pumped his legs. The confusion of not knowing where he was going and what he was running from was staggering.

Finally, having reached an area covered in grass and without holes, Uko fell to his knees in momentary relief. Looking back over his shoulder revealed wafting plumes of smoke. He crawled backwards, further away from the field of pits. He expected something or someone to lunge forward and grab him. Nothing did. His heartbeat slowed as he got back to his feet and turned away from the craters. In front of him stood a massive iron gate that had not been there when he first arrived. There was nothing to the right or left of it. He cautiously approached it, peeking over his shoulder to make sure he wasn't being followed.

A sign hung over the middle of the gate several feet in the air above Uko's head:

Isle of the Dead

Uko looked around in hopes of finding another gate with a sign that said something happier. Unfortunately, he was stuck with this gloomy doorway. He placed his hand on the cold gate, took a deep breath, and pushed. The gate didn't budge. He shoved even harder, but it still did not move. He stepped back, looked back up at the sign, and wondered why he was trying so hard to get into a place called Isle of the Dead. But since there didn't seem to be any better options, he futilely tried pushing the gate open again. Finally, he closed his hand and gently knocked.

He heard an even gentler knocking coming from the other end, as if someone was on the other side mimicking him. When the knocking stopped, he knocked a little harder. He paused and leaned his ear to the gate to see if he could hear another response. After a moment of silence, the gate was yanked open, causing him to stumble forward. He barely had time to brace himself before hitting the ground. When he looked up, he was struck by the sudden brightness of the sun above him. It shone so brightly that he had to squint his eyes. While he did, the silhouette of a person stepped in front of him.

Uko pushed himself away from the silhouette, and tried to use his hand to block the sun's glare so he could get a better look.

"Don't worry," Uko heard as his eyes began focusing on the person in front of him. He could see a boy with his hands in his pockets. "I'm not gonna hurt you."

Uko slowly stood up as his eyes adjusted to the light. The boy was a little taller than him, with an average build. He wore a black letterman jacket with gray arms and the word "Raiders" stitched across the front. He didn't smile or even extend a hand of greeting, but simply stood there and stared as Uko turned to see that the gate that he'd just fallen through was now gone.

"Where are we?" Uko asked as he looked at whirling smoke behind him.

"We're dead," the boy replied.

Uko snapped to attention. "What?!"

"We're dead," he repeated without changing his inflection. "This is the Isle of the Dead. I'm your tour guide. My name is Nasir. Nice to meet you."

CHAPTER 8

Isle of the Dead

"What do you mean we're dead?" Uko asked, his voice shrill with worry.

"You died in Pangea. This is where you come when that happens," Nasir said. "What happened to you? Did you fall off a cliff or choke on food or something?"

Uko thought back to the wedding and Slim's betrayal. "I was stabbed."

"Oh wow. That's interesting," Nasir said, eyebrows raised. "By who?"

"Chief," Uko replied. He paused and watched Nasir's face to see the expected change in expression—the dawn of recognition—but there was no response. "The leader of the Coyotes," he added.

"Never heard of him."

"Oh," Uko said as he cocked his head back. "Okay."

"So can I do my job as your tour guide now?"

"Sure."

"Great." Nasir carefully turned around and pointed to his feet. As Uko looked down, he realized that Nasir's toes hung slightly over the edge of a cliff that Uko had never noticed. His eyes widened.

"Come here," Nasir quietly said over his shoulder.

Uko stepped cautiously and stood a few feet behind him as he took in the sight. It was difficult at their height to breathe in the cold, thin air. From their vantage point, Uko saw that the cliff they stood on was part of a mountain that extended to his left. To his right, there was nothing but black water that rippled with each burst of chilly wind. Directly in front of them, the tops of tremendously tall fir trees swayed silently. Even though their place on the cliff had to be thousands of feet above the water, some of the trees extended above their heads.

"We're at the top of Kelu Mountain. It's shaped like a horseshoe that surrounds those trees in front of us," Nasir calmly said. "The water down there is the sea that surrounds this island."

Uko turned and stared out at the water again. "We're on an island?" he said to himself.

"Of the dead," Nasir replied. "Don't forget that part."

Uko shuddered. "I'm not *dead* dead though. I'm dreaming. I just need to wake up, right?"

"Yeah, that's true," Nasir said slowly. "But waking up is the hardest part. I've seen people waste away on this island while they try waking up. Have you ever felt yourself partially awake but not really?"

Uko thought to himself and recalled vague memories of lying in bed both half awake and half paralyzed with sleep. Even the memory of the feeling didn't sit well with him. The sensation was so vulnerable and helpless it terrified him.

"Yeah, I think so," Uko replied.

A slight smile glided across Nasir's face. "They say there's a demon sitting on your chest when that happens. It's trying to suffocate you."

Uko's eyes widened. "Are you serious?"

Nasir didn't answer. Instead, he turned back to the cliff.

"So how do I wake up?" Uko finally asked.

"There are only two ways. The first way is if you just wait until you wake up. At some point, your body will try to wake up on its own. It won't be fun, though," Nasir said. "Waking up from the Isle of the Dead is extremely stressful. That's when you have that demon sitting on your chest."

Uko nodded his head. "Okay, what's the other way?"

"You escape from the island," Nasir replied. He stood in silence as Uko looked on for more information. After a moment, he pointed out toward the sea to their left. "Do you wanna try and escape the island?"

Uko opened his mouth but couldn't put an intelligible word together. There was something about Nasir's demeanor that was off-putting. Or maybe it was something he said. A word.

Escape.

That was it. Everything in Uko took notice of Nasir saying "escape" the island instead of "leave." Although he wasn't sure how he knew, Uko was certain that word was chosen for a reason.

Nasir extended his hand to Uko in an exaggerated handshake motion.

"Yes?" he asked. "Do you want to do it?"

Uko looked at his hand and felt the regret of his decision before even making it. *It's either this or some freaking thing sitting on my chest. I don't have a choice.*

He whispered "okay" and reached out to shake Nasir's hand. Instead he gripped Uko high on his forearm by his elbow. Before Uko could understand what was happening, Nasir pulled him into an embrace and patted him on the back with his other hand.

"Let's do it," Nasir finally said after ending the hug and stepping back. "Follow me. It's gonna be hard work, though. We can't waste time."

With that, he stepped off the cliff. Uko yelled out in a mixture of astonishment and fear at what looked like an apparent suicide. Instead, he heard the thud of someone landing near him. He stepped forward to see Nasir balancing on a ridge several feet below. As Uko looked down, Nasir was already scurrying toward the center of the mountain. The ridge was so narrow he had to walk sideways like a crab, while gripping the face of the cliff to keep himself from falling backwards. He never slowed or looked back to see if Uko was following. He was off to the races and didn't seem to care who came with him.

Uko took a deep breath and dropped down to where Nasir was. He would have loved to go at a much more leisurely pace, but that didn't seem to be an option right now. After landing, he gripped the cold, jagged rocks of the mountain and attempted to follow his guide.

"Slow down!" Uko yelled. His voice was drowned out by the suddenly loud and vicious wind that whipped the trees around them. To Uko, it sounded like being on the wing of an airplane flying through a storm. His own plea to Nasir sounded like it came from someone miles away. The only thing that registered to his ears outside of the wind was the steady thumping of his heart.

"Can't slow down, bruh. You're doing well," Uko heard. Nasir's voice was quiet yet perfectly clear, as if Uko heard it in his mind instead of from someone scaling a mountain several yards ahead of him.

What the...? Uko thought. *He's not even looking at me.*

"I'm your tour guide," Nasir's omniscient voice replied. "I'm right here with you no matter how far apart we get. Now hurry up because I'm about to jump down again."

Oh my God please no! Uko thought and screamed involuntarily.

"Too late!"

Nasir was down another level of rock in an instant. As his foot landed, he seemed to lose balance and tip backward toward the tree-covered abyss below them. Only a timely outstretched arm that gripped a jutting rock saved him from tumbling down.

"Ha! That was close," Nasir said, wiping his brow with his free hand. "Your turn."

The queasiness in Uko's stomach threatened to boil over and paralyze him. Why couldn't things be easy? Why did it have to be all this?

Nasir chuckled as Uko turned away from the mountain and jumped down another level. His landing was a little more graceful than Nasir's, but it terrified him nonetheless. He looked up the path Nasir was trekking toward the center of the mountain and saw him standing patiently a few yards ahead. Although the ridge was wider and more forgiving of mistakes, the wind was not. It clawed at Uko mercilessly, and he charged forward with a bowed head and squinted eyes. When he finally reached his guide, he plopped down onto the ground next to him. The plateau was slightly depressed into the side of the mountain like the mouth of a shallow cave. It provided a little relief from the barrage of elements around them. Uko panted with exhaustion.

"We're close to the middle of the mountain. We covered a lot of ground. Man, I love those jumps. Go on, look up at where we were before."

"No, I'm good," Uko said. He preferred to spend this time trying to calm his wracking nerves.

"Suit yourself. We still have a little more ground to cover. We have to get to the very middle of the mountain. The middle of the horseshoe."

"Why?" Uko asked. "Aren't we trying to get off the island? Why don't we just climb down?"

Nasir sat down next to Uko and pulled his lanky legs toward his chest. He rested his arms across his knees and stared out into the swirling tornado of rock, tree branches, and debris that swirled in front of them.

"It would make sense to try and climb down, but it wouldn't work. It's a very difficult climb, and I don't think you'd make it. I don't think I would make it if I'm being honest. We'd both probably fall off the side of this mountain." Nasir turned back to Uko and stood up. He extended his hands to help Uko stand up as well. "Falling off the mountain means we die, and dying means we get new tour guides and go back to where we started. The journey to get off the island just gets harder. The wind will be the least of your worries."

Uko started at Nasir with eyes that yearned for more information but a mouth too scared to ask.

"Yeah," Nasir knowingly added. "Let's focus on making the most out of this. In the middle of the mountain, there's a cave that we can use to get to the ground. It's a shortcut."

"Okay," Uko replied. "Let's go."

The boys leaned back out into the elements. Nasir scanned both north and south before waving for Uko to join him. They gripped jutting rock and slowly pushed forward.

"We're coming up to a jump, Uko." Nasir's voice echoed to Uko through his thoughts. "Take your time."

Uko tried to see the jump that Nasir was talking about but couldn't see around him. The guide stopped walking and ducked into an expectant squat. After a few moments, he leaped forward. Now Uko could see the large gap in the path they'd traveled along the mountain. He was amazed that Nasir was able to clear it without a running start.

What the heck? I can't do that! he thought.

"Yes, you can."

"No. I can't."

"Take a deep breath and step back a couple steps so you can get a running start. You got this."

Nasir motioned him over, and Uko closed his eyes, steeling himself. *You got this, you got this, you got this*. He repeated the phrase again and again as a mantra. His eyes shot open as the usual howling of wind was cut by a distinct scream. He turned just in time to see a figure tumbling down the giant trees to his right. The scream somehow got louder even as the person vanished into the dark mass of trees. Uko's eyes widened to the size of dinner plates.

"Don't worry about them. Some people fall. That won't be you," Nasir shouted. "You got this, you got this, you got this. Keep repeating that, and let's go."

Uko shook his head and tried to clear his thoughts. He opened his eyes again and looked at the gap between him and Nasir, which seemed even wider than before. He walked several paces back and shrugged his shoulders. *All right, let's go.* He charged forward. As he got to the edge of his side of the ledge, he leaped with all the strength his legs could muster. With the effort, he came close enough to land chest first on the edge of Nasir's ledge. The hard rock knocked the wind out of him as his legs swung under. Nasir scrambled to grab both of his arms. The pain he felt nearly matched the shock of not making the jump and the terror of feeling himself slip.

"I got you," Nasir audibly screamed as he tried to pull Uko up. "I got you. Don't worry. Pull!"

Coughing with effort, Uko did. His shirt ripped, and the rocks cut through his jeans, but he managed to climb onto his feet on the right side of the gap. He panted in exhaustion and excitement.

"You did it," Nasir said, patting Uko on the back. "I told you. I told you."

Let's just keep going, Uko thought. Nasir nodded and turned back toward the center of the horseshoe.

"You got heart," Nasir said. "You're gonna need it."

The boys continued their journey along the unforgiving mountainside cliff, moving in silence. From time to time, the sound of another person's scream in the distance would threaten to rattle Uko's nerves. But despite that, they kept moving forward, wordlessly helping each other past jutting rocks, loose stones, and wind-whipped tree branches.

After some time, Nasir turned to Uko with a look of concern.

What is it? Uko thought. *Are we here?*

Nasir nodded.

They stood near the edge of another cave in the center of the mountain. Uko walked by Nasir to get a better look. The entrance was partially lit but dimmed to pitch black a few steps in. Uko turned back to Nasir, trying to figure out what caused the change in his demeanor.

What's wrong?

"I'm scared," Nasir said. "This part is different."

"Different how?"

Nasir looked into the darkness of the cave. "Worse."

CHAPTER 9

Woman on the Boat

A chill shot through Uko's body as he took another measured step into the cave. Nasir straightened and readied himself before stepping in front of Uko.

"Walk right behind me. You're not gonna be able to see anything. Try your best to not freak out," Nasir whispered.

"Okay," Uko said. "What makes this worse, though?" Nasir was more worried about this after they'd almost died on the side of a mountain? That seemed like a bad sign.

"We're just going to exchange thoughts till we get out. No words. We have to be as quiet as possible," Nasir replied through the same eerie inner voice that sounded as if he spoke through a speaker in Uko's head. "There's other people in here. We don't want them to know we're here."

What?! Uko frantically thought. *What do you mean there's other people here? Where?*

Before he replied, Nasir began inching forward. Uko was forced to place his hand on his back and creep forward as well. "Remember how I said this was the shortcut that leads you to the bottom of the mountain?"

Yeah.

"There's other people who've come through here and didn't make it. They gave up. They're still here."

Where? Uko thought as he looked around in vain. *Where are they?*

"You're not gonna see them. But they're definitely here. If your heart wasn't beating as loud as it is, you'd probably be able to hear them."

Uko did feel the thump of his heart throughout his body. The thought of not being alone in the heavy darkness made his skin crawl. *What do they want?*

"To stop you from getting through. They never made it so why should you?" Nasir replied. "That's human nature, ain't it?"

As they slid their feet deeper into the cave, Uko could feel the temperature around him warm. The draftiness of the cave's entrance gave way to an unsettling heat—the body heat you feel in crowded rooms. He didn't like it.

"Listen," Nasir said. Although Uko stopped in fear the moment Nasir spoke, he continued to hear footsteps around him. The sounds rose and fell everywhere he turned his blinded eyes.

Is that them? Uko thought before he felt the sensation of someone brush against his arm. It was as light and innocent as someone passing you on a busy sidewalk. Down here in this foreign world, it felt ominous. Uko immediately imagined some creature reaching out to grab him. He opened his mouth to scream and felt Nasir's hand clasp over it.

"NO!" he felt Nasir yell within him. It was too late. The momentum he brought to keep Uko from yelling pushed him down and freed him from the protective grab. As he landed loudly on the cave ground, Uko yelled out in a combo reaction to the pain and fear of the moment. "AHHHHHHH!!!!"

Uko felt arms pull his body up. "Great. Now we gotta run. Let's go. Right now!"

Uko stumbled to his feet and gripped Nasir's arms as tightly as he could. As he got up, he felt the swipe of another hand graze his back. The once partially silent and pitch-black cave was now alive with sound. Uko could see figures scurrying in different directions as puffs of light jumped around their bodies.

"At least the light they create when they run makes it easier to see," Nasir audibly yelled back at Uko. They dashed through the crowd that quickly closed in on their location. They rounded corners at full speed and pushed their way through bodies. The people who were previously shrouded in darkness now lit up like fireflies as they swarmed around them. Even though they moved incredibly fast, things felt slowed down for Uko at times. Every few moments he would feel the tug of someone on his shirt or his leg, and he'd have to turn to push them away. The cloudy light would illuminate a young boy's face, or the wrinkled arm of an old woman. Uko would reach out clumsily while running and somehow get them off of him without tripping over himself.

"Almost there!" Nasir screamed. "Almost there."

Uko craned his head around Nasir's frame to try and get a better look at the light at the end of the tunnel. Instead, all he saw was the bright light caused by four or five people running toward them.

"Oh no!" Uko screamed as his feet clipped Nasir's, and he lost his balance. The stress of so much running and dodging caught up to him. His outstretched hands barely saved him from a mouthful of cave dirt as he crashed into the ground. After landing, he looked up in time to see a massive swarm of light engage with Nasir and then fall away.

"Get up, Uko!" he heard a voice scream. "They're gonna grab you."

Uko flipped onto his back, light sparking around him. The bodies of two people standing over him were frighteningly clear. As he tried to get his arms up in time to protect himself, he felt hands pull them violently. He couldn't see what grabbed him, but he knew all hope was lost. He was captured by these people, and they would pull him back into the cave to spend his days doing the same to others. He closed his eyes again. Hopefully it wouldn't hurt.

"Get up, man. Get up."

Uko's eyes reluctantly opened. Nasir stood above him with an outstretched hand. Uko grabbed it and pulled himself up. He felt so disoriented that it seemed like the world was appearing piece by piece around him.

"They got us?" Uko asked. He noticed rough pillars behind Nasir, tall hairs under his feet, a dim glow above the two of them.

"Nah, I couldn't go out like that. I pulled your scary self out," Nasir replied with a chuckle.

There was the bark of a tree behind Nasir, tall grass under his feet, the glow of stars above them.

"Are you serious?!" Uko nearly yelled. "We made it?"

"Yeah, man," Nasir solemnly said. "My first time ever making it."

"They've caught you before?"

"No. That's the first time I ever tried to even go through the cave. I've heard about the shortcut a million times, but I've never had the guts to give it a shot. Normally I try the long way down, and it never works."

"What made you do it differently this time?"

"I don't know," Nasir said. He paused and surveyed Uko. "Something different about you. Felt like we could do it. I was wrong, though."

"What you mean? We did make it!"

"Because of me," Nasir laughed. "I saved your butt, Mr. Passed Out."

"Shut up!" Uko said with a slight prickle of embarrassment.

"I'm messing with you, man," Nasir assured him. His face reverted to his solemn look. "You did good. Especially since you didn't know what you were getting into. Kinda brave."

Uko blushed. "Thanks." They stared forward in silence. "So now what?"

The world around them was now clear to Uko, and it wasn't very inviting. They were surrounded by imposing tree trunks atop rocky patches of grass that grew from white sand. Uko looked up to see the shape-shifting stars and moonlight that flitted down to them through the treetop branches.

"This is all new to me. This is the center of the Isle of the Dead. Like I said, I've never been this far. I've never gotten off the cliff," Nasir replied. He bent down to examine the peculiar grass that jutted from soft sand. His hands rubbed the thick roots that crissed and crossed all around their feet.

"So we gotta get off the island to wake up, right?" Uko said. "Let's figure out where the water is."

"Sounds good to me."

Nasir silently pointed in a random direction, and Uko shrugged. They began their quiet walk through the weave of trees in search of an exit. Thanks to the otherwise silent air around them, the distant sound of lapping waves acted as a compass. They helped each other through tight spaces and over fallen trees.

"Where you from?" Uko asked after a few moments of strenuous trekking.

"Oakland. But I go to school in Maryland. Freshman."

"You're in college?"

"Yup."

"Cool. I'm from Newark."

"Cool."

Uko nodded quietly while he tried to think of a way to keep the conversation going, but could only repeat *Cool* in his head. Nasir offered no additional tidbits of info. As awkward as Uko felt in the silence, Nasir seemed right at home. After what seemed like an eternity, they arrived at what looked like a wall in front of them. They cautiously approached it, and as they got closer, Uko realized that it was more like a curtain made of vines. The green and dark blue plant ropes hung down from above, forming a twisting, tangled barrier that kept them from moving forward. Uko placed a trembling hand on a vine and half expected it to writhe in response. When it didn't, he looked back to Nasir for advice on what to do next. Nasir only stared back with wide eyes. Uko put a second hand on another vine and pulled them apart. There was so much resistance, it felt like they were glued together. It wasn't until Nasir stepped in and assisted in the prying effort that they were able to tear apart an opening large enough for a searching head to poke through.

As the boys pried the hole open, the silence they were so used to was interrupted by the loud conversation of what sounded like dozens of people. Uko immediately yanked his hand back in fear of being seen, but the gap remained, and the words flooded in. They were hard to make out since there were multiple conversations happening all at once.

"You will never find another like that—"

"Never, sir. Never—"

"Inside the boat. I can see—"

"Tired. So tired—"

"Silence!"

The final word cut through everything and was repeated multiple times in excited whispers.

Silence, silence, silence, silence.

Uko held his breath. Nasir backed away, and as Uko looked to him, Nasir turned to dart around in search of an exit. Uko placed a hand on his shoulder and put a pointed index finger to his mouth.

"Hello?" a voice called out from the clearing beyond the vines. Uko tried his best to look through the hole without being spotted, but could not. He again looked to Nasir; his deer-in-the-headlights expression didn't help.

"Hello?" the voice called again. It was sweet and innocent. "Who's there?"

"What do we do," Nasir asked quietly. Uko couldn't decide.

"Please show yourself," the voice called out again.

Uko looked back at Nasir. "We don't have a choice."

"What?! What do you mean?" Nasir replied.

"We're gonna get out," Uko said with the confidence that kicked in when times like this occurred in Pangea. "It's my turn to get us to the next step. Come on."

Before Nasir could reply, Uko put his entire head through the opening in the vines and pulled himself into the clearing. As soon as he did, his heightened senses were hit from all angles with the sudden change. The grassy white sand they walked through before was now jet black. Uko turned back to the wall

of vines behind him to see Nasir step out after him with an awestruck look. There were more voices, now screaming with excitement.

"Yes!"

"Two of them!"

"Almost done—keep going—yes—never sir, never—Silence!"

The voice stopped, and at that moment Uko noticed the flickering colors of light on his skin. He looked up to see that the dark sky filled with lights was completely different. Like a wall-to-wall IMAX movie theater screen above his head, everything he looked up at was a vision of another world. It was daylight, and he could see a wall and roof above him. He looked to his left and saw his familiar bedroom dresser with Kanju sitting regally atop it. He looked to his right and saw the face of his annoying brother Femi looking down on him. He gasped. The unfamiliar voices were replaced with Femi's.

"Stop playing and wake up. We're late for school." Femi's face came closer to the sky vision that Uko was gazing into, until it was so big Uko could count his nose hairs.

"Uko!"

Uko saw the face back up and then saw a hand reach down toward him. Suddenly the black sands under him, trees behind him, and water before him shook violently. Uko yelped and looked to Nasir, who didn't seem affected by the sudden earthquake. He stared up and screamed into the air, "Don't take my stuff, Sean!"

"Uko! What are you doing?!" Femi's voice boomed. "Ew! Are you sleeping with your eyes open? Yo! What's wrong with you?"

"Femi!" Uko cried out, but Femi's larger-than-life face didn't register it. Instead, another hand flashed across the sky, and the ground quaked again.

After a few moments of rocking, everything settled. Nasir continued to stare upwards, and it seemed he was experiencing his own vision.

"Come aboard the boat to get back home." A voice cut through the noise. Uko's head spun in its direction, and he saw a tall woman in a cloak standing at the front of a long and narrow boat at the edge of the water.

"Who are you?" Uko asked shakily.

"Come aboard the boat to get back home," the voice repeated. This time Uko recognized the sweet voice he heard earlier. "You and your friend."

Uko looked back to Nasir, who was now sitting cross-legged with his head in his hands.

"Nasir!" Uko yelled out. Nasir looked up with teary eyes. "Do you see the boat?"

He nodded.

"She said we gotta get on it," Uko said as he ran over to him. "Let's go."

"This whole thing's creepy as hell, man," Nasir said as he looked back at the sky. "I'm not gettin' on no boat."

"Come now. I'm leaving," the woman's voice effortlessly called out. Uko turned to see her turn her back to them as she stuck a massive oar into the water. The boat started slowly floating away from the shore.

"Nas, let's go!" Uko pleaded. He wasn't sure whether it was the best decision to run toward this stranger, but he couldn't think of any better alternatives.

"Uko! I'm gonna call Mom," Femi's voice boomed again.

Uko looked back down at Nasir, who returned his head to his palms. "This is too much. I'm not goin' nowhere," Nasir said.

"Come!" the woman called out again.

"Uko!" Femi yelled.

"Nas!" Uko screamed. He reached down and pulled his reluctant partner up. "We gotta go, bro. I got you."

He put an arm around Nasir's shoulder and began running toward the boat, now a few feet away from shore. They splashed through waist-deep water to get on board, but as they got closer, the boat picked up speed. Uko pumped his legs into the water with Nasir, and the boat only got farther away. The waves became rougher and rougher as they ran toward the woman.

"Walk to me," the woman said without turning back. Even though she was the farthest she'd been, Uko heard her clearly.

"No! This is crazy. I'm done," Nasir said.

"Come on!" Uko yelled back, his frustration and confusion somehow fueling his determination. He stopped stomping through the water and stood still with Nasir. "Just do it. Let's go home."

To Uko's surprise, Nasir calmed down enough to stop moving. When they were completely still, and the boat seemed to be at the horizon, Uko stuck out a foot. With Nasir under his arm and a lump in his throat, he slowly walked toward the boat. The gap between them and the boat closed incredibly fast. They sank and sank until they had to tilt their eyes to the sky to keep water from overtaking them. Against all logic, the water didn't rise any higher. Before they realized the gravity of what they were doing, they were at the edge of the boat. The woman reached out to them, and Uko grabbed it and pulled himself and Nasir over the side.

"Oh my God!" Nasir yelled. "We did it! We did it!"

Uko was at a loss for words. He looked up to the woman as she turned back toward the horizon, sticking her oar into the water. The waves calmed, and the sky darkened again.

Drained and elated, the boys laughed before closing their eyes in exhaustion.

CHAPTER 10

Greetings from the Griot

The room shook like it was recovering from the detonation of a silent bomb. Femi's face was now joined by that of Uko's equally concerned mom.

"Coco Bean!" Uko's mom shouted. "This isn't funny anymore. Please stop. Can you hear me? Wake up."

Their eyes were locked with his as he tried in vain to raise a comforting hand to calm everyone. The weight of an invisible lead blanket kept him pinned to the bed. His eyes could dart around, he could feel, he could hear. But he couldn't move. He tried to scream, but his face remained frozen.

"Bro, come on, man," Femi pleaded.

Uko strained against the invisible blanket—nothing.

"Baby."

His eyes darted around in search of an answer—nothing.

"What's wrong, Uko?!"

Then, suddenly and without explanation, the blanket dissolved, and the weight lifted. His hands shot up, and his brother and mother yelled.

"What happened?" they asked in unison.

Uko's mind flashed back to the sign he'd read.

Isle of the Dead

He shuddered at the memory of fighting his way out with his tour guide Nasir.

"I don't know," Uko replied before hugging them. "I'm fine now."

Later that morning, Uko and Manny walked to the city bus stop near the end of their block. It would be their first solo ride to school and should have been a celebration of approaching adulthood. Instead, Uko was in his head.

"What's good with you?" Manny asked.

"Huh?"

"I said, what's good with you?"

"Oh, I'm good. Just tired. Didn't get a lot of sleep."

"Why?" Manny's eyes narrowed.

"Nothing," Uko replied. He considered going through the play-by-play with him, but remembered the less than enthusiastic reaction he got the last time he described a tough Nightmare Detective assignment. The novelty was gone, and it was hard to have his friends believe something that only Uko experienced.

The bus arrived and tossed a cold puddle of morning rainwater at their feet as it skidded to a stop. They climbed aboard, dug in their pockets for change for the fare, and sauntered to the back. The seats were filled with the lowered heads and sleepy eyes of adults headed to jobs around the city.

"You got a plan?" Manny asked as they sat down. "For Op Mongoose?"

"Oh yeah. I didn't even think about that. Look at who's hyped about it all of a sudden. You stay up all night thinking about it or somethin'?"

"I'm only doing this because of you. Something's off about that dude, Brandon. But new school, new adventures, right?"

"You right. And it's John Henry, remember?"

"Whatever. If I learn how to make a Pac-Man game, then this will all really be worth it."

"You ain't gonna learn how to make nothing," Uko chuckled.

"Keep hating. I'll be the one to figure out the school has a secret society. AND I'll find time to code two games. Sleep on me if you want."

Uko leaned his head back and snored loudly, until an older woman in the seat in front of them turned around and shushed him. Manny laughed into his cupped hands.

❖ ❖ ❖

"Good morning, students," the voice on the classroom loudspeaker droned. "Be aware that tonight is Back to School Night. All families are expected to arrive at 6:30 PM. Please speak to your homeroom teacher if you have any questions."

"Shoot," Uko said under his breath. With the excitement of yesterday, he'd forgotten to remind his folks. He turned to Manny and whispered, "Did you tell your parents about tonight?"

"Yeah. They can't make it, though."

"I forgot to tell them. I don't know if they can come."

"You out here messin' up left and right."

"Leave me alone."

As the morning announcements ended, the students jumped to their feet as they made their way to their classes for the day.

"Who you got?" Manny asked while looking at his printed schedule.

"I got Mr. K—Social Studies."

"Oh, good. You're lucky. I got Mr. Penns. I hope he's not boring."

The boys dapped, and Manny headed out of the room. Then Uko spotted Brandon up the hall, looking at him with a big smile on his face.

"What's good, Anansi?" he said as he reached Uko. "How you feeling?"

"What's up, John Henry? I'm good."

"You sure?" Brandon said as he leaned in to examine Uko more closely. Uko got a sudden urge to randomly jump into a discussion about Pangea. He quickly decided that probably wouldn't be a good idea.

"Yeah, I'm fine. I was thinking about Operation Mongoose last night," Uko lied.

"Yeah?"

"Yeah, I think you're onto something. Can you imagine how people are gonna react when Last Word breaks the news because of us?"

"Yes!" Brandon shouted and pumped his fist before pointing at Uko in silence while smiling. "You're right. It's gonna be wild."

"Wild," Uko repeated.

"You coming tonight, right?" Brandon asked.

"To what?"

"Back to School Night. You forgot already?"

"Right. Yeah, I think so. I gotta text my folks later to see if they're free."

"Cool, let me know. Maybe we'll be able to snoop around a little. Take my number," Brandon said as he pulled out a pen to write in the notebook he held. He tore the sheet out and handed it to Uko. "When you get to your phone, make sure you save that and send me a message."

"Got it."

Brandon hummed as the boys parted. Uko stuffed the paper in his pocket and headed toward Mr. K's class. The bell signaling the start of class rang as he arrived and slid into an empty desk.

Mr. K was writing on the board. Even though he hadn't said anything, the class quieted in anticipation as the bell finished ringing.

"Good morning, guys. Glad you made it to class just in time," he said as he looked at Uko. Uko tried to apologize, but Mr. K waved it off. "Let's get started, shall we?"

Mr. K's words sounded miles away. Getting up early today in order to make the bus was catching up to Uko. His eyes felt heavy, and the warmth of the room felt inviting. Before he knew it, his chin was on his palm.

I'll just rest my eyes for a few minutes.

"That's a great idea. Great idea," Uko could hear Mr. Kittles say to the class as he drifted to sleep.

❖ ❖ ❖

From his vantage point, Uko could see four or five people seated on cots around him in the dark room. The air was heavy with the smell of a doctor's office in need of a deep cleaning. The men and women who occupied the cots looked like the grizzled military types Uko saw in movies he watched with his dad. Uko watched them replace bloodstained cloths on their arms and legs with what looked like fresh gauze. Uko wished he could evaporate into thin air or transform into a tiny mosquito that could fly far from this place without being seen.

"The contract isn't up for another two months, and we're dropping like flies," one man on a crooked cot snarled to himself.

"What do you expect? They don't pay your family all that money to knit," a woman near him replied.

"Yeah, I guess," a second man said from across the room. He marched over to a door to their right and stood still as dusty smoke spilled over it.

"The mayhem continues," the woman said.

"The mayhem continues," the first man echoed with a heavy sigh. He got up and stood next to the man near the smoking door.

"Don't get captured," she said.

Without warning or the control to stop himself, Uko sneezed. The entire room turned to him in unison. If eyes could conjure laser beams of anger, the eyes on him would have done it.

❖ ❖ ❖

Uko's chin banged against his desk, and he bit his tongue. He yelped and threw a hand over his face as he heard a collective gasp around him. For a second or two there was silence as he opened his eyes to see everyone else's eyes fixed on him. The moment he realized he had just woke up after falling asleep in class, the entire class broke out into laughter and finger pointing.

"Class! Class, settle down," Mr. K said from the front of the room. "Calm down, everyone. We still have work to complete. Are you all right, Uko?"

"Yes," Uko lied. His tongue was throbbing, and his pride was even more badly bruised. He looked down at his desk and the drops of drool on it.

"Let's talk after class," Mr. K added. The dying fits of laughter were now replaced with excited and childish "oooohs" from around the room. "Cut it out, guys."

When the school bell rang, and the kids spilled out of the class, Uko remained seated with his eyes fixed on his desk. Mr. K quietly walked up to him and sat on top of the desk in front of Uko.

"Sorry I was boring you so much," he said to Uko with a small smile.

"No, you weren't. Really, you were great. I don't know what happened. I just fell asleep," Uko replied. "It won't happen again."

Mr. K nodded his head. "It's fine. It happens. You have a tough time getting to sleep last night?"

"No. But I had to wake up early," Uko replied. "It won't happen again."

"No worries," Mr. K replied. "You see anything interesting?"

"See anything?"

"When you fell asleep today in class. Did you have any daydreams? I always daydream when I nap in the middle of the day."

"Oh," Uko replied. He considered the question, and for a second thought about telling the truth. No, it would be best to say less and end this awkward exchange. "No, just fell asleep."

Mr. K hummed an acknowledgement but kept his eyes on Uko with his head cocked to the side. "Nothing at all? That's no fun."

Uko looked up at Mr. K. "Well, a quick daydream."

Mr. K's eyes lit up. "Yeah? Well, let's hear it. Hopefully it was more exciting than my speech."

"No, you weren't boring. I promise."

"I'm joking. Go ahead. Tell me about the daydream."

"Um," Uko said while trying to decide how to describe what happened. "I don't know. I imagined I was in a room with a bunch of people who looked like they were hurt or something. And then they saw me and then the next thing I know, I'm awake again."

Mr. K nodded quietly then asked, "Did you know them?"

"No. Never seen them before."

"That's weird."

"Yeah."

"Okay," Mr. K said. He abruptly stood and walked to the back of the class, picking up stray papers left by students. "One of these days, I gotta tell you about *my* daydreams," he added with a laugh.

"Sure," Uko said. He got up and started for the door. "I'll see you tomorrow then."

"Sounds good," Mr. K responded while picking something up. "Can you put your textbook back on my desk before you go?"

"Sure."

Uko swiped up the textbook he was given at the beginning of class and placed it on top of the pile of other books on Mr. K's desk. Before he turned to walk away, a word stood out to him on the desk. As he turned back to get a better look, Mr. K called out to him from the back of the room.

"You see something interesting?" Mr. K asked.

"I'm sorry. I was being nosy," Uko said. "I didn't mean to stare."

"No, it's fine," Mr. Kittles said as he walked up to his desk. "I know it's not these textbooks. What is it?"

Uko pointed to a black and white composition notebook he saw sticking out from under some other binders. The word on the corner of its front label caught his eye.

Griot

He placed a finger on the book, and Mr. Kittles pulled it out from under the rubble.

"Oh, this?" he said, while glancing at it the way you would a favorite old T-shirt. "Not sure how this got up here." He handed Uko the book and sat on the edge of the desk while Uko read the handwritten title.

The Oral History of Pangea
Volume I
By The Griot

Uko couldn't believe what he was seeing as he opened the old notebook to inspect it.

"Looks like it might be a student's creative writing assignment or something," Mr. Kittles added. "Probably a 6th grader. The handwriting's so sloppy."

Uko couldn't keep his thoughts straight. After months of wearing the pages out of Volume III of the Oral History of Pangea notebook he found in the library, he was now holding the first volume. Mr. K continued speaking, but Uko didn't even hear him as he skimmed through the pages and saw the familiar setup—Name, Date, and Story. He felt like hugging someone.

"You think it was a kid who goes here that wrote this?" Uko asked.

"It's possible," Mr. K replied.

"Can I have it?"

"Really?"

"Yes, please!"

After a short pause, Mr. K replied, "I don't see why not. Just don't tell anyone I gave it to you. I don't want anyone saying I gave away their journal."

Even though he quickly regretted how childish it made him look in the moment, Uko squealed with glee when he got the okay.

"Hurry, you don't want to be late for your next class, Uko."

"Okay," Uko said as he turned to walk out.

"I hope you enjoy the book," Mr. K added.

"I will."

CHAPTER 11

Birth of a President

Uko buried his head in the notebook as he hustled to his next class. Should he just look at the dates and names and then come back for the stories? Should he read it in order? Would it be better to start at the end? He flipped the pages madly while jogging down the hallway, before he slammed into what felt like a brick wall. The book smashed against his face, and he stumbled back onto his bottom. He looked up at the last person he'd want to literally run into outside of class.

"What are you doing?!" Simms yelled at him.

"Sorry. I'm sorry. I wasn't paying attention," Uko stammered.

Simms reached down and pulled Uko onto his feet with a surprisingly little amount of effort. Even as Uko stood, he was several inches shorter than him. Simms' grip on Uko's collar was like a vise. As if beating him in Mr. K's class wasn't enough. Now he had to add to the list of offenses.

"You messed up my sneakers," he said. "You gonna pay me for them?"

Uko tried to think of something to say that would get him out of this without committing money he didn't have.

"How much?" Uko asked.

"For these Jordans?" he said. The question seemed to make him even angrier.

"Oh, I didn't know that's what they were."

"Simms!" someone yelled out from down the hall. "What on earth do you think you're doing?"

Simms immediately let go of Uko, who promptly stumbled onto his other sneaker by accident. They both looked at the hall to see the Principal Walker marching toward them.

"Both of you get to class immediately," Principal Walker added.

"Sorry for the other sneaker," Uko said as he picked up his notebook and scurried away. Simms turned back to him with a look so angry it made Uko glad the principal was still in the hallway with them.

Uko got to his next class a few moments after the bell had rung. He quickly grabbed a textbook from the front and moved to a seat in the back of the room. As the lesson started, and the teacher up front went through the usual "first class of the year" introductions, Uko couldn't lift his head from his new prized possession, the Griot's Notebook. He looked through the pages with pleasure as he tried to find a story to land on. Finally, he decided to go with one near the center. He glanced back up to the front of the class to make sure he wasn't missing anything important. When he saw that the teacher was beginning a boring story about when she was in 6th grade, he began reading.

Loretta Hansberry - July 26, 2016 8:12AM

I was always an observant person. I wasn't the person who led every conversation or always had something witty to add. I didn't need to know you for a long time to know when you were about to lie, or notice that your eyes were sad even though you were smiling and pretending to be happy. Some people say it's being able to read vibes but I don't know if it's that mystical. We're all a lot simpler than we pretend to be. I think that's what helped me stand apart—I really listened. I really looked at people. I read people and their actions. Does that make sense?

I was the same way in Pangea. I watched more than anything and I loved it. I learned how to jump dreams by watching someone else who probably didn't even realize I was staring at them from a distance. From there, you couldn't stop me. I was able to be in a dream of mine and immediately find a person there that was different - a person that my mind didn't make up. I could spot a Pangean from a mile away. I'd just go up to that person and start a conversation. If I got a nickel from all the surprised looks I've gotten from people by doing that! I was always reading the room.

I've been in dreams with some of my Waking Life neighbors. You think you know someone because you've lived around them for years, but share a dream with them and see how your impression changes. I've made so many friends in my dreams - real life celebrities, athletes, politicians, world class chefs, royalty. They tried to count it up a couple years ago and said that I've been in contact with more than twenty million people in Pangea at this point. I know I've been doing this for years but even I find that number hard to believe. But who knows, you probably don't get this many people obsessed with every word you say if you haven't been in the dreams of twenty million people.

"Twenty million people?!" Uko repeated aloud without realizing it.

"What was that, sir?" the teacher up front asked. Uko felt the heads of twenty students turn toward him and his sudden outburst. His cheeks flushed.

"Nothing. Sorry," he replied.

"Okay, let's try to keep it down," the teacher replied before returning to the discussion that Uko ignored, continuing to read through the notebook.

Later that day when Uko's lunch period began, he mindlessly gathered his food in the lunch line and chose a seat by himself at an empty table in the back of the cafeteria. Hunched over and in the zone, he read story after story between bites of his hot dog.

"Is it any good?" Uko heard someone close to him say. He looked up to see Manny and Brandon sitting at the table with amused looks on their faces.

"He sees us now," Brandon chuckled.

"When did you guys get here?" Uko asked.

"We've been here for like ten minutes. We wanted to see how long it would take before you realized it, but then I got tired of waiting," Manny replied.

"Sorry," Uko said as he closed the notebook and put it under his tray.

"What is that? You studying on the first day of school?" Brandon asked.

"No," Uko replied. "Mr. K gave it to me. It's a notebook that he had on his desk. He wasn't sure where it came from, but it's like a journal or something." Uko looked at Manny and without words, showed him the notebook on his lunch tray. He knew Manny would recognize it, having the same name as the one they found in the library last summer.

"It was on his desk?" Manny asked in amazement.

"Yeah," Uko said.

"Let me see it," Brandon asked.

"No," Uko said a little too forcefully.

"All right bro, calm down," Brandon replied. "I guess I won't tell you the plan for tonight then."

"What plan?" Uko asked.

"Yeah, what plan?" Manny added.

"We're gonna take our first crack at getting info for this Coding Club story. Er, Operation Mongoose. My fault," Brandon replied.

"How?" Uko and Manny both asked.

"I just said I'm not gonna tell you the plan anymore. What do I look like explaining it now?" Brandon replied. "Just make sure you're both here when it starts, and figure out a way to get away from your parents for ten minutes when I'm ready."

Uko dug in his pocket for his cell phone to see if either of his parents had responded to his last-minute reminder about Back to School Night. His dad's annoyed response let him know that he would take him.

"How are we gonna know when you're ready?" Manny asked.

"Put your numbers in this. I'll text you," Brandon said as he handed Manny his phone. Manny entered his number before handing it to Uko to do the same. Brandon got up with his tray of uneaten food and tossed it into the garbage before returning and getting his phone back. "Thanks for the numbers. I'll see y'all later."

Manny and Uko exchanged glances with each other. "Why did you even get food if you're not gonna eat it?" Uko asked.

"Gotta keep up appearances, Anansi," Brandon said as he pulled a cereal bar from his pocket and walked away.

"He's mad weird," Manny said.

"Yeah, he is," Uko added.

"We gonna go through with it?"

"We gave him our number, Duende. I guess so," Uko replied as the boys laughed.

"So the notebook that Mr. K had is the same one we found in the library?"

Uko slid the book back out from under his tray. "Not the same one but close. It's Volume One. The one I have is Volume Three. All the dates are older, so that means this is definitely a thing. Maybe the Griot is still writing them."

Manny flipped through the notebook. "Maybe. I wonder how he got this."

"Yeah, I wonder too."

"Excuse me, can I sit here?" said a voice that interrupted their conversation. They looked up to see a tall girl standing in front of their table with a tray of food.

"Sure," they both replied.

"Thank you," she said as she sat and placed her tray down. "My name is Adriana."

"Hi. I'm Manny, and this is Uko."

"Nice to meet you," she said as she extended her hand. Both boys clumsily shook it. "You guys are sixth graders, right?"

"Yeah."

"That's nice. I was scared too when I first came to middle school, but you're gonna love it here."

"We're not scared," Uko protested.

"Okay, maybe not scared. You're just new," she said with a smirk. "It's a big change, but you don't have to worry about it. Just put yourself out there and try out for stuff and meet people. It works."

"Okay," Uko replied. He had to keep his face from showing his annoyance with the "just be a go-getter" advice. He didn't need a pep talk in the middle of lunch.

"What did you do to meet people?" Manny asked. Uko turned to him with raised eyebrows.

"I joined different clubs. That was fun. Some I ended up quitting, but at least I tried," Adriana replied. "But the biggest thing for me was running for class president. I did that in sixth and seventh grade and won both times. I'm gonna take a break and just relax for eighth."

"What was it like running for class president? What did you do?" Manny asked. Uko was amazed that he was keeping this conversation going.

"I was nervous at first because I didn't know anybody," she said as she tucked her hair behind her ear. "I walked around and introduced myself to people and told them I was gonna run for president. I made flyers and I put them up all over the school. And I killed it in the debate."

"Wow," Manny said. Uko stared at him but Manny wouldn't return his look. "What did you do as a president? What's that like?" Manny added.

"Oh my God, it's sooo much fun. You meet with your grade advisors—I think Mr. K is the advisor for sixth—and you talk about things you can do for the other sixth graders. You represent them. Then at the end of the year you help plan the class gift. It's awesome," Adriana said to Manny. It was as if Uko wasn't there anymore.

"That sounds cool. Right, Uko?" Manny said. Uko squinted his eyes at him in reply.

"You would make a great class president, Manny. You're so inquisitive," Adriana said. "You should do it."

"Really?" Manny said. "What do you think, Uko?" he added without actually turning to look at Uko.

"I can help. An eighth grader and former president on your team can't hurt," Adriana said. She pulled a small mirror from her pocket and looked at herself. She pouted her lips a few times before putting the mirror away when she seemed satisfied. She looked over her shoulder at a group of girls by the cafeteria exit. "I gotta go."

"Yeah, definitely. Okay," Manny said.

"Think about it, all right?"

"Yeah. Yeah, definitely," Manny replied. Adriana got up and joined the girls. The group walked out of the room as the bell signaling the end of this lunch period sounded. After staring at the door for a few seconds, Manny turned back to Uko and his still squinted eyes.

"Wow, my guy," Uko said slowly. "Just...wow."

"Shut up," Manny said as he punched Uko in the arm. "I think I'm gonna run."

"Yeah, I can tell," Uko replied, earning him another punch. The boys got up to empty their trays. "As long as you're here for Operation Mongoose tonight then I'm good," Uko added.

"What are you talking about?"

"Oh my GOD, Manny!"

"I'm kidding. I'm kidding!"

CHAPTER 12

Back to School Night

When the boys returned to school later that night, the air was filled with the nervous energy of performers prepping for a concert. Dozens of parents and kids strolled into the school in clusters of conversation and laughter. Since Manny's parents were both working late, the boys arrived with Uko's dad. They followed the directions of the cheerful staff to the auditorium to join the other families for the principal's introduction. They both kept their phones clutched in their hands in anticipation of Brandon's text. In the time since school ended, the only plan they could come up with to leave Uko's dad when the text arrived was to hope an opportunity presented itself to them. Uko had little faith in the non-plan.

In the auditorium, families took their seats on the bleachers while faculty and staff stood on the basketball court floor. The boys took a seat near the top of the bleachers in order to get a good view of everyone else. As the people watched, Uko tried to identify which group each student belonged to based on what they did—the cool kids who apparently changed outfits just for tonight, the sports kids, the after-school club kids, the smart kids. Uko had a good idea of where everyone fit in the Robeson Middle social world. As Manny tapped him and pointed out Adriana, Mr. Walker took his spot at the podium at the center of the court.

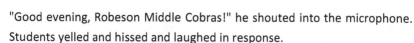

"Good evening, Robeson Middle Cobras!" he shouted into the microphone. Students yelled and hissed and laughed in response.

"We're super excited here for another school year. The teachers were just telling me how bored they were with their summer vacations," he added. "Tonight, we want to introduce the incoming sixth graders to the school and show everyone what we have planned for our students this year. We pride ourselves on doing something new each and every year, so even you eighth graders will learn about something interesting we have planned. I won't keep everyone long. Parents, you can walk with your students to their classrooms and speak with their wonderful teachers about what's on the horizon for this fall. If you have any questions, feel free to reach out to any of us. And as always, Go Cobras!"

As the students in the crowd erupted into another chorus of hisses and cheers, Uko's phone buzzed in his hand. He looked down to see that Brandon had messaged both him and Manny in a group text:

Meet me outside the computer room in the basement. Make sure you're not followed :)

Uko looked back up to Manny who mouthed "How?" to him. He shrugged in response.

"Where we off to first, gentleman?" Uko's dad asked while looking at one of his brochures.

"You guys go to our homeroom class," Manny quickly replied. "I'll go to my Spanish class teacher in the basement before it gets crowded down there. I'll meet up with you guys after."

"You sure? I told your mom I wouldn't lose you."

"Yeah, I'll have my phone."

Outside of his dad's view, Uko nodded to Manny to show how impressed he was with the improvised plan.

"See ya Ooks," Manny said before descending the bleachers and heading out of the auditorium. As he exited the room, he turned back to Uko with an exaggerated smile and thumbs-up that made Uko chuckle.

"So let's check out these teachers," Uko's dad said as he looked down at the list of classrooms he received when they arrived. "How about we start with your homeroom teacher, Ms. Givens? You lead the way."

Uko descended the bleachers with his eyes on the bustling group of parents and students going in different directions. As he got to the floor, he was tripped by an outstretched foot. He fell awkwardly, groping at empty air and slamming to the ground. Half the auditorium erupted in laughter as he turned over on his back and looked up to see that the culprit was Simms. Simms smiled, gave an animated shrug, and asked, "What happened?" He could barely hold back his laughter as humiliation set into Uko's bones.

"Hey!" Uko's dad yelled as he grabbed Simms by the shoulder and spun him around. "What's your problem?" he snarled into the boy's startled face. Uko's jaw dropped at the flash of aggression from his normally mild-mannered father. Before Simms could reply, Mr. Kittles rushed in and held Uko's father's arms while escorting him out.

"Let's all take a second and step out this way," he said as he rushed past Uko, who jumped up and joined them. Uko looked back over his shoulder to see the crowd look as stunned as he felt at the entire spectacle. Mr. K walked with Uko's dad into an empty classroom by the auditorium while his father huffed loudly. When they entered the class, Mr. K quickly closed the door and turned back to the group.

"You okay, Uko?" he asked.

"Yeah," Uko said through rapid breaths.

"What about you, Mister..."

"Hill," Uko's dad replied.

"Mr. Hill. Are you all right? I know things got a little heated out there. I'm Mr. Kittles," he said while smiling and extending his hand.

"I'm really sorry about that. I don't know what got into me. I just—"

"No apologies needed. Cory Simms can be a jerk," Mr. Kittles interrupted. The moment broke up the tension with light laughter from everyone.

"Do you know that kid?" Uko's dad asked Uko.

"Kinda. I mistakenly ran into him in the hallway earlier today and messed up his sneakers. I guess he's getting me back for that," Uko replied.

"Getting you back? What type of mess is that? I want something done about him," Uko's dad shouted to Mr. Kittles.

"I understand, but I don't think it's going to be an issue. I'm sure he's going to get his due punishment and will move on," Mr. Kittles replied.

"How can you be so sure?" Uko's dad asked.

"That's usually how these things go. One kid feels like he needs to get back at another for something silly, and then they get in trouble for it and move on. But regardless of what happens, I'll watch out for Uko. You've got my word."

Uko's dad looked from Uko to Mr. Kittles in silence as he considered.

"Okay then," he said as he shook his hand. "I appreciate that."

"No problem," Mr. Kittles replied. "Well, I gotta go speak to parents, so I'll leave you two so you can get into even more trouble. If you want to talk, I'll be in room 232 upstairs. Otherwise, I'll see you tomorrow, Uko."

"Thanks again," Uko's dad said as Mr. K stepped out of the room. When he closed the door, Uko's dad turned back to Uko.

"You all right?" he said.

"Yeah, I'm fine," Uko replied. "All this time I thought you were Bruce Banner, and it turns out you're the Incredible Hulk."

Uko's dad leaned back, laughing. "I don't know about all that. I just hate when people mess with my boys. Especially if they didn't do anything to deserve it. You didn't deserve it, did you?" he added with a smile.

"Nope. Just minding my business."

"Good. Well, keep your head down, stick with Manny, and get your work done. Some kids have their own issues and they want to take it out on you. Ignore all that noise."

"Will do, Daddy."

Uko's dad hugged him and playfully messed up his hair.

"Oh, and maybe you don't mention this to Mommy," Uko's dad added as he approached the door to exit the room.

"I thought you were a tough guy. I was gonna text Mommy and let her know that you beat up kids now."

"Keep messing around," Uko's dad replied with a twinkle in his eye as he opened the door, scanned the hall, and turned back to Uko. "You won't like me when I'm angry."

As Uko traveled from class to class with his dad, he kept glancing at his phone for a text from Manny or Brandon. What type of trouble could they have gotten themselves into? Did they discover something really cool? It ate away at him as he listened to welcome speech after welcome speech from his music teacher and gym teacher and homeroom teacher. When Uko's dad would ask if Manny was all right, Uko would lie and say that Manny had texted and said he was fine. The last thing he wanted was to cause a scare that would make them search for Manny early, potentially catching them in the middle of something they shouldn't be doing.

Toward the end of the night, Uko decided to finally send a **What are you doing?** text to both Brandon and Manny.

"Where is Manny?" Uko's dad asked the moment the text went out, as if his parental intuition could sense Uko's concern.

"I just texted him to say we're gonna leave soon," Uko replied. While he spoke, he felt his phone vibrate to let him know he'd received two messages.

Manny: We're done. Meet you by the main staircase. - Duende out
Brandon: John Henry here. Mission accomplished! ☺

A shot of excitement rushed through Uko, and a cheesy smile spread across his face. "Manny said he'll meet us by the front."

The hallway back to the front of the school was filled with curious faces that whispered to each other as they stared at Uko and his father. When they arrived at the stairs, Uko saw his dad scan the crowd for Manny while avoiding eye contact with anyone. Maybe he was just as uneasy about what happened in the auditorium as Uko. At least he didn't have to come back to school tomorrow and deal with people talking about it constantly.

"Hey, guys!" Manny called out to them as he approached from the stairs that led to the basement. "You guys got here quick."

"You ready?" Uko's dad asked.

"Yes, Mr. Hill. Got all my Welcome-Backness in. Ready to go home."

Uko looked at Manny with eyes pleading for even a sliver of information. Manny softly shook his head no and placed his arm around Uko as they walked out of the school.

In the car, Uko could barely get his seatbelt on before he was questioning Manny on what he and Brandon found. Manny laughed and glanced at Uko's father in the driver's seat to make sure he wasn't listening. When he felt like the coast was clear, he began recounting their adventure.

"When we got to the computer room, someone was in it."

"Who?"

"Not sure. You know that utility closet that's down there next to the class? We ducked into there and hid with the door cracked open so we could see what was happening."

"Both of you?"

"Yeah. So, while we were waiting—"

"Isn't that a tiny closet?"

Manny rolled his eyes and ignored the question. "While we were waiting, we saw the person come out, but they had a hat on really low so we couldn't see their face. Whoever it was, it looked like a woman. She locked the door and left. We waited a few seconds and then we came out. I thought we wouldn't be able to get into the computer lab since it was locked, but Brandon pulled out his student ID and slid it between the doorjamb and doorknob. He told me to be on lookout and the next thing you know, he got the door open."

"Wow! So you guys broke in?"

"Uh, yeah. I guess so. But we're doing it for good, though."

"Mmm-hmm."

"Anyway, we kept the lights off so no one would notice, and we looked around with our phone camera lights."

"And what did you find?" Uko asked with anticipation. His voice was nearly in a whisper as he leaned in.

"Laptops. A whole bin of them in the back."

"Laptops?"

"Yeah. Brand new ones. And there was a list of teacher names in the bin too. Some names were crossed out, some weren't, and some were highlighted. And we found a Post-It note at the bottom of the bin that said 'Don't mess this up.' It looked like it was Principal Walker's handwriting."

"How do you know that?"

"His 'welcome back to school' notes to everyone were handwritten."

"So you're a handwriting expert now?" Uko was disappointed with the news. He'd expected something much more explosive. "All you found were laptops?"

"Yeah." Manny looked confused by Uko's question. "You don't see it?"

"See what?"

"Brandon said the school never has money for anything. So there's no way they got an entire bin of brand-new laptops for no reason. And we think that the person who was there before we went in is the one who dropped them off. Who was she? Why did she do it after school when Ms. Kowalski wasn't around? Plus, she LOOKED sketchy. Then there's the list of teacher names with numbers next to each one. Some are highlighted and some are crossed out."

"Yeah, that's probably just the list of teachers who are supposed to be getting the laptops."

"A note from the principal saying don't mess this up? I don't know for sure, Ooks, but this might be something more."

Uko was skeptical. "Seems like you're stretching."

"We're home, boys," Uko's dad interrupted from the front seat as the car pulled into Uko's driveway. "Manny, tell your parents we said hello. Mrs. Hill told me she and Femi had a good time hanging out with Carlos while your parents were at work."

"Thank you, Mr. Hill," Manny replied before turning to Uko. "I'm not saying it's a definite but maybe something's up. Doesn't hurt to try and find out."

"It might," Uko replied.

"We'll see. I took a picture of the note and the teacher names. We'll talk about it tomorrow. Have a good one," Manny said as everyone got out of the car.

"All right, man," Uko replied quietly. He didn't see things the way that Manny and Brandon did, but the thought stuck with him. It might be a crazy conspiracy and a waste of time. But what if they were right? The idea of them finding out some secret they weren't supposed to know even existed both thrilled and frightened him. What if this really was something deep?

Visions of FBI operations and secret societies swirled around Uko's head as he lay in bed that night. Whatever the truth was, he hoped they wouldn't get into trouble in the process of finding out. Or if it was something dangerous, he would be able to convince Manny and Brandon to stop before they did.

It's just teacher laptops, he thought to himself as he drifted to sleep. *That's all it is. Nothing more.*

CHAPTER 13

Returning Favors

Uko stood near the familiar resting log in the enchanted garden of his dream limbo. He took time to admire the quiet stillness. Being here was not a given every night. There were several nights where he wouldn't dream at all. Instead, he would just close his eyes in bed and then wake up the next day. No dream jumping, no Nightmare Detecting, nothing. Those nights were the worst. He'd rather go through a terrifying nightmare in some strange part of Pangea than not have anything happen.

As he walked through the meadow toward the dark forest that led to his DreamHub, he crouched down and touched the tips of the tall grass with his fingers. The beads of cold dew always brought pleasant chills. He sensed a flicker of motion ahead of him, and his eyes darted back up toward the forest. Not too far away, a figure walked between the trees. He stopped in his tracks. The shadow of the trees obstructed Uko's view. After a few moments, it was clear the figure was a person, and after a few more moments it was clear the person was a boy. He walked to where the forest edge met the meadow grass and stood perfectly still. The two boys stared at each other for several moments before Uko began tentatively walking forward.

"Who is that?" Uko asked cautiously. There was no reply. Uko continued to approach, taking shallow breaths. "Who are you?"

Nothing.

As Uko got close, the boy stepped forward out of the shadows of the trees. The sun finally struck him. As recognition began to hit Uko, the boy spoke.

"It's Nasir. Remember me?" he said softly. Uko's mind instantly placed the voice and face. The quiet college-aged kid from the Isle of the Dead was somehow waiting for him in his dream sanctuary.

"Yeah I remember," Uko replied as he came closer. His eyes scanned Nasir and the area around him for hidden threats. "What are you doing here?"

"It's all good," Nasir replied, showing Uko both of his empty palms. "I'm not tryna hurt you. I just wanted to talk."

"About what?"

"About that dream last night. On the Isle of the Dead," Nasir calmly responded. "You saved me back there."

Uko raised his eyebrows. "I think it was the other way around. I would have never made it out without you," he replied. "You were a pretty good tour guide."

Nasir looked at Uko in silence for a few moments before smiling. "What are you up to?"

"What do you mean?"

"You doing anything right now?"

"I was just gonna go see if I can jump into some dreams. I told you I was a Nightmare Detective, right?"

"No, I don't think you did. How is that?"

"It's good. I'm pretty good at it. Always love dream hopping and helping different people."

Nasir stepped to the side and gestured toward the Silk Road path into the center of the forest. "After you."

Uko stared at him for a moment as he tried to read his intentions. His blank expression seemed neither welcoming nor particularly dangerous.

"How did you get here?" Uko asked as he started walking down the path with Nasir beside him. Uko realized that the only other person that has walked down this path with him was Toni. He sighed with the thought.

"Us tour guides end up having pretty tight dream connections to the people we help. Especially if we get them off the Island. Once I learned your dream address, I figured I'd come here and say thanks."

"Oh, okay."

"So tell me about Chief."

Uko raised his eyebrows again while looking to Nasir. "Do you know who he is?"

"I might."

"When I brought him up the first time, you looked like you had no idea what I was talking about."

"I didn't know you back then. Now I'm getting to know you."

"Oh yeah? How am I doing so far?"

Nasir laughed softly. It was the first time Uko saw him do more than a mild smile. "Tell me how you know Chief," Nasir asked again.

"I met him when I was becoming a Nightmare Detective. He visited me in a dream on this subway train. He said he liked to meet the new recruits. Then he tried to convince me to join the Coyotes instead," Uko said. He looked up to the sun, which had become more and more blotted by tree branches as they approached the center of the forest. "When I told him no, he got really mad and has had it out for me ever since. During my last Detective test, he was there. He tried to sabotage it."

"I'm guessing you passed anyway?"

"Yeah."

Nasir nodded slowly again as he strolled with his hands cupped behind his back. "So how did he kill you?"

"I met someone in a dream I was working who gave me a gift I thought would help me stop Chief forever. But it turned out to be a trick."

Nasir tilted his head up. "What was it?"

"Some special box. He called it the Watch of Nana."

"What did the man look like? The man who gave it to you."

Uko searched his memory for the man he met in that secret bar. "He was big. Really big. Said his name was Charles Slim. I was there to help him in his dream, but then he said he wanted to give me something special and brought up the watch thing."

"Did he tell you to use it on Chief?"

"No, that was my idea. He just described what it could do. He said I could freeze whoever I wanted in the box forever."

Nasir nodded again. "Well done."

Uko looked at Nasir carefully. Now that they were closer to the DreamHub, it was getting harder to see his face in the dark. "What do you mean?" Uko asked.

Nasir looked back at him with silent, unblinking eyes before speaking. "That man works for Chief. He's a high-ranking Coyote. I'm surprised they sent him. Chief must really have it out for you."

Uko stopped walking. "How do you know all of this? Are you a Nightmare Detective?"

"No, never was."

"Are you a Coyote? Is this another trick?"

"No. But I wouldn't say yes if it was so that's not really a helpful question," Nasir said. "Here in Pangea, I'm in what you'd call Intelligence."

"Intelligence?"

Nasir started walking down the Silk Road again. "Yeah. People like me find out secrets. Either for ourselves or for people who pay us."

"Who are the people who pay you?"

"Different people," Nasir replied. He looked at the expression on Uko's face. "Mostly good."

Uko began looking around the forest warily. He suddenly got the feeling that they weren't alone. Nasir continued.

131

"In the Sleep Waking world, intelligence is crucial. You have people in organizations like the CIA or the FBI who spend their entire lives collecting information that can swing a war. Or can keep a war from starting in the first place. The same thing happens in Pangea."

"So are you a part of the CIA or something?"

"No, I do it on my own. I prefer to freelance. But there are organizations in Pangea that you've probably never heard of that do it for specific causes." Nasir gently put a hand on Uko's back and guided him to continue walking. Uko fought the feeling that he was being led to his death.

"Listen, I'm not involved in any of that. I just thought I could stop Chief. I definitely don't want any problems," Uko said with a tremble in his voice.

"It's fine, I'm not gonna give you any problems. Don't be so worried all the time," Nasir said. "I like you. I figured I could return the favor for getting me off the island." They reached the center of the forest where Uko's DreamHub would spill from the treetops and light the pitch-black space with lavender and silver clouds of fog. With an uneasy feeling, he tried to pretend that the DreamHub didn't exist and thought of ways to try and make himself wake up. But within a few moments, the portal to Pangea appeared like clockwork. Uko sucked his teeth in anger and heard Nasir chuckle to himself.

"Why do you want to get rid of Chief so badly?" Nasir asked. His face glowed with the warm light of the Hub's fog. "And why does he hate you so much? You're just a kid doing that Detective stuff. Y'all can both just ignore each other."

Uko took a moment to consider the question. "I don't know. I never thought of it like that. I just feel like he shouldn't get away with the stuff he does," Uko replied. He turned to Nasir as the dark images in the foggy clouds cast weird shadows on their faces. "People kept telling me he was big and bad and I should just let it be. But I figured someone should stop him. So why not me? You know?"

Nasir breathed in deeply and looked toward the treetops above them.

"How old are you?" Nasir finally asked.

"I just turned thirteen."

"Happy belated birthday."

"Thanks?" Uko replied, wondering where this was going.

"Can I show you something?" Nasir finally asked.

"What is it?"

"I want you to meet someone. That's how I'm gonna pay you back. I'll introduce you to her."

"Who?"

"Ms. Loretta. The person I wanna be one day," Nasir said before placing his hand on his chin. "I guess everybody wants to be her."

"Why?"

"Because in Pangea, she's the only person I've ever heard of who has perfect sight."

"What's that?" Uko asked.

Nasir ignored him and waved his hand over the DreamHub's clouds in front of them. He gazed intently as they scattered. He motioned the fog back and forth as images formed within them then vanished. His hand danced through the fog, pulling things left and right as he arranged it to his liking. "People jump through hoops trying to meet her. Get some sage advice or learn something about a problem in their real life. She rarely does it though. Says it's tiring."

With one eye, Uko watched Nasir swim through the clouds and with the other, he gauged Nasir's face to see if he was messing with him.

"You're friends with her?" Uko asked.

"No, I wouldn't say friends. Just someone who owes me a favor." Nasir answered. "So I'll use it tonight. I know she usually doesn't entertain strangers, but meeting you will be how she pays me back."

"Why does she owe you?" Uko asked.

"I found someone for her. Someone she loved." Nasir finally stopped wading through the clouds. He looked at the images before him like a painting he was pleased with and nodded. To Uko, it looked like random blotches. "There it is," Nasir said to himself before turning to Uko. "Let's go."

Uko took a deep breath, trying to figure out what he should do next. His mind searched for an answer, but nothing came to him. Nasir silently watched him as he tried to decide. Finally, Nasir spoke again.

"I know what you're thinking, but trust me. It'll change you."

Uko looked at Nasir's face and his hard-to-read blank expression for a moment, before nodding his head.

Nasir stepped forward into the fog, and Uko followed.

CHAPTER 14

Finding Ms. Loretta

As the familiar white light faded, an ocean of cars and motorcycles weaved together in front of him. In every direction, there was a stream of traffic that flowed without direction or guidance. Uko noticed a motorcyclist take a moment to look up at him in confusion, and Uko realized he was sitting on top of a traffic light. A bolt of fear tore through him. He was about to fall onto the hundreds of motorists below him zipping at top speed.

"You good?" Nasir said behind him. He turned his head carefully to see Nasir on the traffic light as well, sitting comfortably.

"No, I'm not. What are we doing up here?"

"Getting to Ms. Loretta. We gotta get across this big street to that field over there." Nasir pointed to an area of low grass at the edge of the swirling mess of cars. On each side of it, apartment buildings and sidewalks covered every spot where there wasn't a car moving too quickly for its own good. As he examined it further, Uko realized that the low grass was the manicured courtyard of an apartment complex. There were modest patches of greenery fenced off by walkways for residents. In the middle of it all was a small playground for children with multicolored swings and a giant frog. Around the entire complex were tall, uniform apartment buildings which reminded him of the daunting project buildings he knew from his hometown.

"How are we gonna do that?"

"Jump down. Hop from car roof to car roof until we get there," Nasir replied casually. Uko turned his head a little more in his direction. He was still fighting the feeling that he was going to tip over.

"Are you joking? This isn't funny."

"No, I'm serious. It's the only way to get over there. And we gotta get there. Unless you have a better way."

"Why didn't we just appear on the grass when we used the DreamHub to get here?"

"Ms. Loretta isn't someone looking to have visitors all the time. You think she'd let it be that easy to get to her?" Nasir replied. He watched Uko quietly for a few moments before speaking again. "Breathe deeply. Calm down and slow down your environment."

Nasir's words made Uko realize he was on the verge of hyperventilating. He took a dramatic gulp of air and held it until his lungs and eyes burned. Then he sipped his breaths and tried to count slowly. The sounds died down, and the cars moved like they were plodding through thick molasses. As Uko opened his eyes and took in things around him, they blurred in and out of vision.

"There you go, bruh." Nasir's words lazily drifted to him. "Now jump before you change your mind."

Uko did. Before thoughts of doubt got the better of him, he slid off the beam directly into the jammed street below. The thud of landing awkwardly on a car roof heightened his senses. He briefly peered into the frightened eyes of the driver through the windshield that separated them. The car swerved, but somehow everything moved slowly enough for him to maintain his balance and composure.

"Keep going, bruh," he heard Nas' voice dreamily waft to him from up ahead.

Nasir fell onto a moving van's roof on all fours before dashing ahead onto the next car. Uko turned his sights to the one after that. He leapt forward and landed on the trunk. Luckily, the cars continued to weave between each other at pace slow enough for Uko to navigate.

"Hurry before it speeds up," Nasir yelled back.

Uko used his hands to balance himself before leaping to the next car and then to the next. With each jump he felt like he was in complete control.

When he finally arrived safely on the other side, Nasir was waiting for him with all smiles.

"Welcome, Mr. Uko. It took you long enough," Nasir said playfully. As he said it, Uko heard the once quiet world crank its volume back to a roar as the traffic behind him picked up again.

"I've never done anything like that. How did we slow time down?"

"Beginner's luck, I guess."

Uko looked at Nasir skeptically. He seemed so overly secretive—even when a simple answer didn't seem like it would hurt. Instead of pressing him further only to be ignored, he quietly followed him to one of the tall buildings at the end of the courtyard. As they walked, Uko saw residents stream in and out of the buildings as they went about the warm summer day in peace.

"So Ms. Loretta lives here?"

"For now. She moves around a lot."

"And she can control who comes to visit here?"

"It would be nice to have that control, but no one does completely. That's why even Ms. Loretta, the Oracle, has to move around so much. When a location gets too familiar for people, or when the wrong people know how to get close, you gotta move and fall off the map again. Only a few people should ever know where you are at any given moment, and those people need to be your day ones."

Uko envisioned a small old woman with bodyguards who shuttled her around Pangea in a wheelchair. Maybe there would be some mystical fog around her, and they'd need a password or something to enter her presence.

"What are we doing when we get there? What's the point?" Uko asked. He was answered with silence. Uko decided to take the opportunity to take in his surroundings. The small playground he'd spotted from on top the traffic light was filled with little kids screaming their hearts out in playful delight. A colorful frog statue spat a fountain of water into the air every few seconds, and the kids ran back and forth underneath its blast.

A pair of men pushing laundry carts engaged in heated discussion near a sign that read "Welcome to Marcy House". As Uko and Nasir passed them, they stopped speaking to gaze at the two boys.

"You need to walk a little faster," Nasir called back to Uko. In his people-watching, Nasir had pulled further ahead of Uko than he'd expected. He skipped forward to catch up to his mute tour guide.

"Do you know people here?" Uko asked.

Nasir stopped and looked around. "Why? Is someone watching us?"

"Those two guys," Uko looked back, only to see they were gone.

"Who?"

"I coulda sworn they were right there."

"Let's just go. Stay close to me," Nasir said before turning back to the path ahead. They reached the entrance to the building at the back of the courtyard. Its heavy metal door looked like it had been built with plans to defend its residents from some future war. Instead of fiddling with the dirty intercom to its right, or looking for keys to open it, Nasir just stood to the side and waited. Uko followed suit. He looked through a window into the sparse lobby of the building. The room—all grimy cinder block walls and dark brown tile—seemed weirdly empty for a day that saw so much activity everywhere else in the courtyard.

"We're just gonna wait till somebody comes out," Nasir said quietly as if he'd anticipated Uko's question. Uko nodded and looked back into the lobby. Still empty. He turned back to the bustling courtyard and leaned against the building.

"What do you do every night in Pangea? How do you spend your time?" Uko asked.

Nasir continued looking into the lobby. He sighed deeply but didn't answer. Uko kept trying.

"Like, I'm a Nightmare Detective and I do the whole dream hopping thing. And before that I just dreamed and that's it. Didn't know that all of this existed. But now that I do, being a Detective kinda gives me meaning. You know what I mean?"

Silence.

"What does that for you?"

Nasir turned his head towards Uko. Uko took it as a small opening and pounced.

"In Pangea. What do you value or think is right?" Uko added.

Nasir sighed again and looked back into the lobby. "Maintaining balance," he said just before Uko tried another question. "By any means necessary."

"Balance?" Uko asked.

Nasir stepped to the side as the lobby door violently swung open and a woman and her child came scrambling out. They didn't even notice the two boys as Nasir used his foot to keep the door from swinging closed. As Uko followed him inside, he noticed how oddly quiet the lobby was. The laughing and conversation from outside were immediately smothered when the heavy metal door slammed shut. As he looked around, he saw the rows of metal mailboxes lining the walls, along with the flyers telling residents to do different things, like remember to recycle and attend the community meeting on Friday. At the back of the lobby were two elevators. Uko walked up and pressed the "Up" button with his elbow.

"Which floor?" he asked Nasir.

"Twenty. But the elevator doesn't work. Gotta take the stairs."

Uko turned to see Nasir standing next to a staircase hallway door propped open with a large brick. "Hope you're in great shape," Nasir said as he turned and began walking up the stairs.

The flickering lights above them cast shadows in all directions as they climbed. Occasionally, Uko was startled by the loud bang of a door as someone entered the staircase. The residents stared at Uko with eyes full of suspicion as they passed the boys on their way downstairs.

"Floor Eight, we're almost halfway there, right?" Nasir joked. He must have noticed the difficulty Uko was having in keeping up. "Don't touch anything," he added as Uko finally broke and grabbed the railing as he tried to catch his breath.

"What? Why?" Uko replied as he yanked his hand back and rubbed it on his pants.

"Actually—do whatever you want," Nasir replied without breaking stride.

"Can we take a break?" Uko asked between gulps of air. "I just need a minute."

Nasir stopped and turned to him. "You get one break. Do you wanna do it now before we get halfway up or do you wanna save it?"

"Why does it have to be one break?"

"What's your decision?" Nasir replied coldly.

Without enough information to figure out what caused the weird limitation, Uko decided it would be best to soldier on. He continued pushing up the stairs even as his legs screamed at him in protest. After two more flights, the door that led to the 10th floor swung open, and a woman stepped out to block Nasir's path.

"You need somethin'?" she asked, eyeing them leerily.

"Just walking up," Nasir replied.

"You know somebody up here?" she asked.

"Nah, further up," Nasir said. He looked back at Uko with an expression that was probably meant to relay a message. Uko couldn't figure out what that might be; the pain in his legs was too great.

"What's your name?" the woman asked. Uko saw her right hand slip into the pocket of her leather bomber jacket. She raised her chin defiantly while waiting for the answer.

"I'm Nasir, this is Uko. We're going to visit a friend. Ms. Loretta."

The woman's eyes widened for a second before re-narrowing to a piercing stare. "How do you know Ms. Loretta?"

"From back in the day," Nasir said coolly.

"You all just some babies. What you mean back in the day?" she asked.

"Some Cuckoos learned young," Nasir replied. Uko squinted at the odd phrase.

The woman seemed to appreciate it. She pulled a small flip phone from her pocket and pointed it at the two of them. Uko heard a loud camera shutter as she took their picture. Afterwards she began typing into the phone.

"Y'all better not bother Ms. Loretta," the woman said without looking up from her phone. She pushed past Uko and continued down the stairs. Without looking back, Nasir continued the climb. When they were a few more flights up, Uko tapped Nasir's shoulder and leaned in.

"What were you talking about back there? What's a Cuckoo?" he whispered.

Nasir turned to Uko, but before he could answer, the door at the flight above them swung open. A tall, muscular man with freckles and short, reddish hair stepped into the hallway. Uko noticed the lettering on the wall that said "Floor 20" next to him as he spoke.

"Nas?"

"Nasir, yeah," Nasir replied.

The man smirked and looked at Uko. "What do you need?" he asked both of them.

"I want to cash in my favor. I need to make an introduction," Nasir replied.

"An intro to him?" the man said while pointing at Uko.

"Yeah, I want Ms. Loretta to meet him."

"You mean you want the Oracle to meet him."

"Yes."

"You sure this is how you want to spend your favor? There ain't some old secret you want to find out?" the man asked. He kept his eyes trained on Uko even though he was interrogating Nasir.

"Yeah, I'm sure," Nasir said while looking back at Uko. "I think it's important. The kid is different. Like I was. Back in the day."

The man nodded quietly while continuing to stare at Uko. "Okay, okay. Good. You come with me, Uko."

How did he know my name?

"Nas, you go hang out in apartment 20M for a minute while I bring your boy over," the man added.

"Okay, cool," Nasir said. He turned to Uko and patted him on his shoulder. "Just be yourself, bruh."

Uko walked through the door behind him. He saw Nasir turn to the right and calmly stroll to a cream-colored door that read "20M." When Uko turned back around, the man stood next to him expectantly.

"You nervous?" the man asked.

"Yeah."

"Good."

The two of them walked toward the opposite end of the hall. It was just wide enough for them to move side by side.

"What is the Oracle like?" Uko asked timidly.

"She's something else," the man replied.

"Uh, okay, I guess."

When they reached the door at the end of the hall, he knocked lightly before placing his hand on the doorknob and waiting.

"Not too late to turn back," the man said to Uko.

Uko drew his head back and tried to read the man's expression. *Are you serious?*

Before he could figure out the answer, the man smiled and opened the door. He backed away and gestured for Uko to enter the darkened doorway.

Uko cautiously tried to peer in, but the dark foyer gave no indications of who or what was inside. At the very back, Uko saw the soft glow of a bedroom lamp shining in another room.

A syrupy voice wafted out. "Come on, son. I'm in the back."

CHAPTER 15

The Oracle

Uko walked into the room with his head on a swivel. With every step, he scanned left and right trying to figure out what he was getting himself into. He walked through the empty room, tripped over what felt like shoes, and reached a small hall that led to what he imagined were bedrooms. *Just leave, Uko. Just leave. This is not worth—*

His thoughts were interrupted by a striking sight. Just as he stepped into the dim light of the hall, his eyes settled on a woman. She sat rigidly upright, facing the door across from her. Her head was slightly tilted toward Uko as he rounded the corner. The skin on her face and arms was damp. Droplets of water glinted in the light of the single bulb that hung above her. But as Uko's eyes drifted lower, he noticed that the deep brown hue of her upper body gave way to dark green fish scales. Instead of feet curled underneath her, she sat on fins, as she calmly braided a thick strand of hair draped over her shoulder.

For a moment, all Uko could do was stare. Although she never fully turned to acknowledge his presence, Uko could feel her watch him in silence. Her smile never wavered as Uko waited and watched.

"Come in," he heard that same smooth voice say. But instead of coming from this...creature, it came from the room in front of her.

"What?" Uko asked the woman in the hall.

She didn't reply or look his way. Instead, she continued to braid. "In here," the voice said again. This time it was clearly from the room. "Open the door."

With one last look at the woman braiding her hair, Uko opened the door and walked in.

His eyes took a second to adjust to the light in the even smaller and dimmer backroom. In the center of it sat a plump, older woman with a majestic mane of long, flowing black hair with a streak of silver. She sat behind a white square foldout table. On each side was an empty metal folding chair, as if she were waiting for three more guests. Uko scanned the room but saw no one else. The woman extended a welcoming hand toward the chair across from her.

"Take a seat," she said softly. As Uko did so, she pulled a deck of playing cards from beneath her embroidered robe. She peeled off half of the deck in one hand, the cards crisply snapping under her fingers.

"I've been told that I needed to meet you," she said. "Uko, correct?"

"Yeah, that's me," Uko replied. "I don't know what I'm supposed to be doing here."

The woman looked him deeply in his eyes. After a moment she shuffled the deck and plopped them on the table.

"Cut," she said quietly.

"What do you mean?" Uko said.

"Cut the deck," she repeated while looking up at him. "Have you never played spades before, young man?"

"No."

"Well, you're in luck. I'll teach you. Take some of the cards from the top and put them on the bottom. Like you cut it in half. We'll keep it simple for now."

"Okay," Uko replied, awkwardly cutting the deck. "Am I supposed to meet you to learn how to play spades?"

"Yes and no," she said as she picked up the deck of cards. "Your friend Nasir must think very highly of you. One of the few favors I owe people and he uses his to set up this introduction. To see if I would help you."

"Help me do what?"

"No point in telling you if we're not even sure you're gonna get my help. I couldn't keep my reputation as the Oracle if I was so easily impressed." She patiently rubbed her palm over her chin. She didn't break eye contact and was highly attentive of everything Uko did, taking note of every tick and movement he made. He wondered if she could read his mind.

"You ready to start, love?"

"Okay then," Uko replied. His mind was racing. What kind of help was hanging in the balance and why would he need it?

The Oracle began dealing out cards face down in front of each of the four chairs at the table, as if there were imaginary players to the right and left of him.

"There are usually four players in any good game of spades. You can play with just two, but it's not serious unless you have four people. Each of you get thirteen cards to cover the entire fifty-two card deck."

When she finished dealing the cards, she smiled at Uko.

"Pick 'em up, this is where the fun starts." As she said this and Uko picked up his cards for inspection, the cards of the imaginary players to the left and right of him hovered into the air as well. They floated at what would be the eye level of an invisible opponent.

"Arrange your cards by suit. Clubs go with clubs, hearts go with hearts, diamonds with diamonds, and spades together. Keep your cards close so no one can see them."

As Uko began arranging his cards, the Oracle continued.

"The cards are in order of value. A deuce is the lowest card in any suit, and it goes up through the number ten, then a Jack, Queen, King, and Ace. For each turn, we each throw one card, in clockwise order. The biggest rule of this game is that the card you play has to match the suit that was first thrown."

The invisible player to Uko's right tossed a 7 of diamonds onto the table. Uko scanned his cards and decided to place down his highest diamond, an ace. The unseen opponent to his left threw a 3 of diamonds, followed by the Oracle's 5 of diamonds.

"Once everyone has thrown their one card in that turn, you want either you or your partner to have the highest card on the table," the Oracle added.

"Are you my partner?" Uko asked.

"You're paying attention—good." She paused to let that sink in. "Anyway, the team that had the highest card collects those cards and keeps them. That group of four cards is called a book. In this case, you had the ace of diamonds, the highest diamond. I collect the cards and we have one book. Make sense?"

Uko nodded.

"Any good partnership requires trust and communication. Incredibly good communication. Because we need to bid, or bet, how many books we're going to win before the game starts," she continued.

Uko felt confident enough to jump in with what he thought the solution to the problem was. "So we tell each other which high cards we have and figure out how many books we'll win."

"Nope, that would be talking across the board. Talking across the board is cheating." She smiled at Uko's confusion the way you look at a puppy chasing its tail. "I tell you how many books I think I would win and you tell me how many you think you'd win. That's it. Of course, it would be a lot easier if we could just talk about which cards we had. But we've gotta take a different route. That's the beauty of this part of the game. Learning to speak without making noise."

"I need to let you know what I can win without coming out and saying it," Uko said quietly.

"Precisely," the Oracle replied as a wide smile crossed her face. "I need to pay attention to you. Pay attention to your tone, your eyes, the way you counted your books the last time we bid. A lot goes into us bidding at the beginning of each hand. It takes effort to develop the type of partnership that does it well."

"Got it."

"Have you ever had a great partner?" the Oracle asked as she lowered her cards and looked at Uko intently.

"Me? I've never played this before. Remember?"

The Oracle didn't reply. Instead she cocked her head to the side and pursed her lips.

"Oh, I did," Uko replied after he realized she meant more than spades. "The girl who taught me about all of this, all of Pangea. She was a great partner."

"Toni, right?"

"Yeah. How did you know?" Uko asked. *She definitely can read my mind*, he thought.

"I've heard about her."

"You have?" Uko replied with a slightly embarrassing amount of enthusiasm.

"What made her so great?" the Oracle said in reply.

Uko blushed. He tried to think of all the incredible aspects of Toni that he admired. He tried to come up with a sentence that summed her up without seeming obsessive. Instead, all he could think of was her smile the night she'd asked him to become a Detective. When he looked back up at the Oracle, she slowly nodded her head and looked back at her cards.

"The only time you can throw out a suit that wasn't played is if that suit isn't in your hand anymore. If that happens, things change," she said.

"Spades are the special cards in this game. Hence the name. They're more important than any other suit in the deck. If you run out of hearts and someone plays an Ace of Hearts, and you play a 3 of spades, that's called a cut and you win that book. When you're bidding on your books with your partner at the beginning of the game, keep that in mind."

"Okay," Uko replied. He looked back at his hand. "Why do you owe Nasir a favor?"

"Persistent, I see," she said as she looked back at her cards. "He helped me find out something that really helped me during a low point in my life."

"You needed help?" Uko asked. He had thought she had the answers to everything.

"We all go through something hard at some point. You'd be surprised how much help people need. Especially when they seem to have it all together."

"Do you have it all together now?"

The Oracle chuckled. "Better than before."

The Oracle continued to play as they spoke. Uko did his best to stay focused on the flow of the game while finding out more about her. He quickly collected books as they won them. When the invisible team won, the books floated to them in neat piles.

"What does it mean to be The Oracle? What do you do?"

"I'm not particularly fond of that name. It's misleading. My name is Loretta. Loretta Hansberry."

Uko felt a pang of *déjà vu* as she said her name. *Why does that sound familiar?* "Okay, Ms. Loretta. Why is it misleading?"

"I'm not the all-seeing entity that the Pangean schoolbooks would have you believe. I can see more than the average citizen. I have access to more information. But it's not worth the trouble that it puts me in," the Oracle said with a deep sigh. Her eyes scanned the cards as they zipped onto the table. "Being so guarded all the time. Being hounded for answers to questions I don't want to think about. It's tiring. Why did you cut me? I was going to win the book with my Jack."

"Oh, I'm sorry. I didn't have any more clubs," Uko said as he reached down to take his ten of spades back. The Oracle reached down and grabbed his hand as he picked up the card.

"You can't take it back," she warned. "Once you play it, that's it. You can't take back mistakes."

"Okay," Uko replied. "What should I have done if I don't have any clubs?"

"If your partner is gonna win the book, you throw out one of the other suits. Get rid of those. That's called throwing off. You save your spades for later. You'll need 'em," the Oracle said.

"Okay."

"My turn to interrogate," she said. "Why do you think Nasir spent his favor on you?"

"He was my guide when I went to the Isle of the Dead, and I saved him."

"You saved him when he was your guide?" the Oracle asked with surprise. "That's interesting."

"Yeah. I guess saving him is why he wanted me to meet you."

"The Isle of the Dead is constantly changing. Sometimes it's a big change, sometimes it's subtle. Nasir seems like a person who's interested in solving

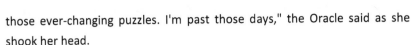

those ever-changing puzzles. I'm past those days," the Oracle said as she shook her head.

"Your name was in the Griot's notebook!" Uko shouted. The memory just connected for him. "I just read it the other day."

The Oracle looked surprised. "You read that? The young man said he wanted to make those interviews famous one day. I guess he did."

"It was in a notebook at my school in real life. My teacher let me keep it. He said he thinks one of the sixth graders wrote it for a project," Uko replied.

"I doubt that. I met the Griot only a year or two ago, and he was very much a grown man. Handsome grown man at that."

"Really?" Uko asked. The Oracle nodded. Now he was even more interested in the notebook and how it got to his school.

"You've quite the inquisitive mind. And you always seem to be in the thick of it. Maybe you have a need for adventure and danger. Your average Nightmare Detective isn't itching to go to the Isle of the Dead."

"Me? No, I would never purposefully go to the Isle of the Dead," Uko replied. The thought sent a shiver down his back.

"You chase danger in different ways. That's the only way to explain a boy your age with a death wish he hopes Chief can fulfill."

Uko sat back. "I don't have a death wish. I just—I'm trying to stop him."

"Why?"

"What do you mean why?"

"Why is it your job to stop him?"

The question seemed so obvious that Uko couldn't figure out how to answer it. He searched his mind for words to describe a gut feeling.

"Because," was all he could muster.

The Oracle stared at him for a while then slowly nodded her head.

"Got it, partner," she finally said. "How do you expect to stop a man that powerful by yourself? While you're playing Rambo, he has an entire network that's ready to die for him. How do you suppose you got fooled by that kind gentleman in that speakeasy?"

Uko's eyes widened. The image of being given the Watch of Nana flashed through his mind. He thought he'd solved the puzzle. Instead, he was sent to the Isle of the Dead by Chief's blade. "You were there?"

"No," she replied. "I did hear about it, though. That whole 'access to information' thing I told you about."

"How does that work? How do you know all this stuff and become the Oracle?"

"Couldn't tell you. I never wanted to become someone that people would nickname and put on some pedestal. I spent my early days in Pangea meeting people. Millions of people. Wake-less nights of wandering and finding myself," she replied. "As you get connected to more people who want to allow you into their life, you build a connection with them. With enough connections, your view of Pangea becomes much fuller. My DreamHub's a busy looking mess that I somehow understand."

"So you have spies," Uko said.

"I have people who relay information to me sometimes. Other times I can see what my closer connections are doing as I gaze into my DreamHub. Which I admit must send off a very Oracle-ly vibe." She laughed. "But it is interesting you brought up the idea of spies. You ever think about doing something like that? Employing spies?"

"No. But that sounds like it might be helpful."

"Terribly helpful."

"Maybe I could do something like that to help with what I'm doing."

"Help with your death wish?"

"It's not a death wish," Uko said, frowning. He sounded less certain each time he said it.

"I'm joking, love. But you're right. You would need help to stand a real chance against Chief," she said. She put her cards down, and the floating cards dropped as well. "How do you plan on doing that?"

Uko smiled. Here was his chance to share his plans with someone who would take everything he said seriously.

"Other Nightmare Detectives. I'd bring us together. Instead of all of us working on our own. Which is what I'm sure Chief prefers."

"A band of fiery kids," the Oracle replied. She folded her arms over her chest and leaned back in her chair. "What else?"

"I need more?"

"Uko, you didn't think that would be enough. This is no simple matter. You need more people."

"Like who?"

"Fighters, allies, mentors," she replied. "Spies."

Uko felt overwhelmed. "How can I find all of those people?"

"Remember why you're here."

Uko smiled brightly. "Are you going to help me?"

The Oracle smiled back. "I'm not going to be out there fighting the good fight with you. But I'll assist in my own way. I'll send word that you have my support, and I'll advise you when I can as you build and lead your team."

"Lead?" Uko replied.

"Yes," the Oracle replied calmly. "This is an effort that you will be the focus of. Nasir brought you here to rally our people to this cause. But you would be front and center. That's the responsibility that comes from my blessing."

Dread started creeping in. Uko was fine with the idea of joining a group that would take on Chief. But leading it? That was much more than he expected. He was not used to the pressure and attention that comes from being the center of anything, much less a fight for a dreamworld.

"You doubt that you can do it?" the Oracle said as she watched him react to what she said. Uko nodded. "Don't be. Nasir brought you here because he saw something in you. The same thing that Chief saw that marked you as his enemy. You care, genuinely, for people and for what's right. That is much rarer than you think. You may feel like you're not qualified to lead this revolution. That's good. The best leaders in history have been those who took charge only reluctantly. We will not let you fail. Absolutely not."

Uko's overwhelming worry gave way to optimism. "Thank you. Thank you so much," Uko said. "I have to thank Nasir too."

"Thank him with work. I'm sure he wanted my blessing over your death wish even more than you," she said with a twinkle in her eye. "He can help build up the group you need to go after Chief. You focus on the Nightmare Detectives, and he can find the others."

"Okay," Uko replied. "That sounds like a plan." He felt himself floating. "Thank you again. I'm going to make this worth your time."

The Oracle stood up from the table and walked to the door that Uko came from. She motioned for him to join her as she held the doorknob, then smiled and patted him on the shoulder. "It's been a long time since I've mingled in the lives of other people in Pangea. But sometimes you find the right partner and things suddenly change," she said. She opened the door a crack. "Never get too old for an adventure."

CHAPTER 16

So Will I

The Oracle led Uko out of the room and back through the dark apartment. The beautiful mermaid, or whatever she was, wasn't sitting in the hall anymore. The apartment was quiet, and the Oracle shuffled along softly as she walked to the front door.

"I'm a little nervous now," Uko said. "I don't know how to start."

"The path will show itself," the Oracle said in a drawn-out voice that sounded like a queen announcing a new law for the land. She turned to Uko and laughed. "I'm pretty good at sounding like an Oracle at least."

She opened the apartment door and stepped out into the hallway. As she waved him out to join her, he felt a pang of shock at just how crowded it was. On each side were people standing silently with their backs against the cinder block walls. Their sheer number was only surpassed by the diversity in their appearance. Uko saw women in military uniforms with pins on their chest and hats held to their side. There were older men with canes and soda bottle glasses that stood at attention. The hallway was filled with small groups of people that represented every walk of life in Pangea. As they lined the walls, they all faced Uko and the Oracle in silent expectation.

"Thank you all for coming on such short notice. I, more than anyone else, appreciate the time of my fellow citizens of Pangea," the Oracle began. She gracefully used her hands for emphasis as she spoke. Uko shuffled between watching her work and staring at the ground. Being in front of such a large group made him too uncomfortable to meet anyone's eyes.

"We are all well aware of the changing morality of this world we all hold dear. Whether it was the violence of lone predators, the corruption of the Cuckoos, or the greed of world leaders—you have asked me countless times to intercede, and I have always declined. This is not because I do not care about what's happening. Quite the opposite. From my viewpoint I've seen crusades for justice start honorably and become tainted. I did not want to be a part, or the cause, of that hurt for someone else," the Oracle added. "But I'm getting older now, and my views are beginning to change. Maybe it is time to step in and do what I can. Maybe it's time to get active."

"I'm all about that action, boss!" someone yelled out from the end of the hallway. A hushed murmur began building through the group. The Oracle waited a few moments before waving the crowd quiet.

"Today I'm in agreement. I believe that as the Neighborhood Watch of Pangea, as you have so lovingly named yourselves, it's time to be assertive," she said. "Stamp out evil at the root, instead of applying bandages. What if we attacked the biggest cause of the pain—the Coyotes themselves."

The whispers in the crowd started up again. Uko looked up to see wide eyes of surprise from some and nods of appreciation from others. The Oracle didn't attempt to quiet them again. Instead, she raised her voice. "This is why I called you here today, and this is why this young man is standing by my side."

The crowd shifted its focus to Uko, and he immediately lowered his gaze back to his shoelaces.

"This is Uko, a Nightmare Detective from Newark. He was brought to me for help without knowing it. And even though he was unaware, I have been a fan of his from afar," she said. Uko turned his head to her in surprise. *She's been watching me?*

"This young man has borne the cross of defeating evil himself for too long. That ends today. I hereby grant the full power and support of my name to the young Uko," she added. The murmurs in the crowd grew again. Uko felt the heat of a thousand eyes staring holes into him. "As you know, I've only done that once before, and the results were disastrous."

"You cannot blame yourself, Ms. Loretta!" another voice shouted out.

The Oracle waved off the encouragement with a faint smile. "I've come to grips with my mistake. In fact, I feel this is quite poetic. The boy I stand with today will be charged with finding and defeating the very man I stood with in this same spot several years ago. The man I gave my first blessing to," the Oracle announced.

Wait, what?! Uko thought to himself. *Is she talking about Chief? Did she do this with Chief before?*

"Not unlike our everyday lives, is it not? Today's courage is always an attempt to make up for yesterday's blunders," the Oracle said as she turned to Uko, pausing to take in his surprise. She turned back to the group and spoke in her loudest voice yet. "Uko has made it his mission to defeat Chief. I have decided to help him till my last breath. Today, I give young Uko my blessing. I ask that you accept it."

The crowd immediately quieted. Uko looked up nervously, unsure what was happening. The expressionless faces didn't give him any hints. The silence made the moment stretch on for ages. After some time, the Oracle turned to him and whispered, "Walk down the hall. If they accept my blessing, they will pledge their support for you. If not, it'll just be you and I."

Uko nodded and began walking. The crowd pushed back against the walls to make a path as they stared. As he reached the first group in the crowd, a hand stuck out and blocked his path forward. Uko turned to the woman in her impressive military uniform as she spoke to both him and the crowd.

"If the seeker of hope stands by him, so will I!" she exclaimed. With that, she knelt and bowed her head. The five women in uniform who stood with her followed her lead. Uko was stunned. He turned back to the Oracle, who smiled back and encouraged him to continue walking.

As he took another step, a man on the other side of the hall reached his hand out and began speaking.

"If the leader of our forces stands by him, so will I!" He knelt on one knee and bowed his head. The six people with him did the same.

Uko was so excited he could barely contain himself. As he continued to walk, the voices came so quickly they nearly overlapped.

"If the protectors of the innocent stand by him, so will I!"

"If the guides of the lost stand by him, so will I!"

"If the advocates for the forgotten stand by him, so will I!"

"If the voices for the voiceless stands by him, so will I!"

"If the advisers of nobility stand by him, so will I!"

With each declaration, another group would kneel as Uko passed them. When Uko got to the end of the hall, the only person standing was Nasir. He waited until Uko got right in front of him before speaking softly.

"I'm all about that action, boss," he said before kneeling. Uko couldn't decide if he was more grateful, excited, nervous, or delighted. Everything rushed through him at once. As Nasir stood back up, all Uko could do was hug him.

"Congratulations," Nasir said.

"Thank you. This is all because of you."

Uko turned back to look at the Oracle but saw that the hallway was empty.

"It's okay. You're waking up," Nasir said.

"But what does this all mean? How do we get started?"

"When we meet again, I'll fill you in. In the meantime, I'll do what I do. See you tomorrow night."

Nasir smiled as he faded away. Before long Uko was back in his room with his alarm clock buzzing.

He heard his mom yell up to him from downstairs. "Get ready for school, Coco!"

❖ ❖ ❖

Uko's mind raced during the entire bus ride to school. Even though it was another dreary day, and Manny fell asleep as soon as they sat down, Uko couldn't contain his excitement. He was chosen. He might not be exactly sure what that meant, but he knew it held some level of significance. If someone as respected as the Oracle and the people in that hall vowed to help him defeat Chief, then how could he lose?

When they arrived at their bus stop, Uko woke up a still exhausted and grumpy Manny. They walked the block to school and entered the building as the swarm of kids scurried in to get breakfast and start their days.

"There he go right there," Uko overheard someone say. When he turned toward the sound, he saw two kids pointing at him as they spoke. The pair immediately turned their attention away and began giggling.

"People are talking about me, Manny," Uko said as they walked into the cafeteria.

"For what?" Manny replied groggily. "Oh, do you think it's because your dad was out here wrestling kids?"

"No, he wasn't."

"I'm joking, fool," Manny chuckled. "But that probably is what they're talking about. I see a lot of people looking at us. I'm sure Simms ain't a fan of the Hill family at all now."

"Great. That's exactly what I needed."

"You'll be all right," Manny replied as they walked through the breakfast line to get their food. After they filled their trays, they sat at a small table in the back where the prying eyes of classmates wouldn't interrupt their meal. "This is a safe school. People talk a big game, but nobody's gonna do anything crazy."

"Mr. Kittles said he'd look out for me."

"So, you straight," Manny said between bites. "I already told you people love him around here."

"Hope so," Uko replied. "Anyway, now that you're fully awake and got some food in you, I can tell you about what happened in Pangea. I met this lady they call the Oracle."

"Who's that?"

"She's a big deal. Almost like a celebrity. I guess she can kind of see everything that's going on in Pangea, and she's crazy connected with people all over the world. People go to her for stuff all the time. But she avoids them. Her people keep moving her around all the time, but this other guy I met named Nasir took me to meet her. And there was a mermaid," Uko said so excitedly he raced through the sentences.

"So you not even tryna have me believe this stuff anymore, are you?" Manny replied.

"I'm serious," Uko laughed. He realized how crazy it all sounded. "She gave me her blessing to try and get rid of Chief. I'm gonna find out how to get in your dream one night so you'll know it's real."

"Be my guest. I dream about video games all night anyway, so you meet me there and we'll just be on the sticks," Manny said. As he did, Brandon crept from behind them and surprised the boys as he slid into a seat near them. Their startled reactions cracked him up.

"I can do this all day," Brandon snickered. "First thing I gotta do is get some creep to you so you learn how to keep track of what's around you. I could have been listening in on y'all while you complained about wetting the bed or something."

"Shut up," Uko replied.

"You got any ideas about those laptops, Mr. Private Eye?" Manny asked.

"Almost forgot about the Case of the School-Issued Laptops for Teachers," Uko added. "Did you find out they have illegally downloaded TV shows on them yet?"

"Hate on it if you want. You couldn't recognize a good story if it sat down next to you at your struggle table," Brandon replied. He pulled out a piece of paper and laid it out in front of the group. "Each of the teacher names have a model number next to them. Whoever assigned these laptops wants to make sure they keep track of exactly who gets each one. On top of that, some of the names are highlighted: Mr. Santiago, Mrs. Lamar, Mr. Kemp, and Ms. Fielder. There's gotta be a reason for that. We need to pay close attention to them and see what they have in common other than being eighth grade teachers."

"Okay, not bad," Uko said. "But how are we gonna keep track of teachers we never see while we're in our sixth grade classes?"

"I have homeroom with Ms. Fielder and math with Mr. Santiago. So I'll keep track of them," Brandon replied. "Uko, you'll watch Mrs. Lamar, and Manny, you got Mr. Kemp. I know you don't have any classes with them, but we just gotta work around that. Maybe you can make friends with some eighth graders."

"That girl Adriana is in eighth grade, right?" Uko asked.

"How do you know Adriana?" Brandon replied with raised eyebrows.

"She came over to talk to Manny about running for class president. Remember, Manny? You said she was flirting with you, right?" Uko teased.

"You're lying," Brandon said. Manny looked like he wanted to crawl into a hole. "Shut up. I didn't say all that. She was just being nice," he replied. "She probably says that to everyone."

"She is nice. But I still don't know why she'd talk to you two," Brandon said skeptically. "I guess we make it work. Try and find out what you can from her without blowing the whole thing up. Can you do that?"

"Speak of the devil," Uko interrupted as he stared at the entrance to the cafeteria.

The boys turned in the same direction and saw Adriana standing there with a bright smile as she looked around the cafeteria. Her hair blew back gracefully as if an invisible fan was beneath her. She immediately spotted the boys and waved at them. They all awkwardly waved back as they wondered if she knew they were talking about her.

After a moment, she waved them over to her.

"Is she talking to us?" Brandon asked.

She pointed at them and then repeated the "come here" wave.

"She is," Manny replied. "I think she's talking to me."

He pointed to himself and mouthed "me?" to confirm. Adriana nodded her head yes and waved him over again. Manny looked at the boys in stunned silence and stood up.

"Guess I'll be getting started on my investigation early, fellas," Manny said with a childish grin. "Don't wait up for me."

CHAPTER 17

Creating a Leader

"What do you think they're talking about?" Uko asked Brandon as they watched Manny rub the back of his neck while speaking with Adriana.

"My friends didn't believe me when I said I knew the corniest kid in the entire school," Brandon said in a voice mimicking Adriana. "Yeah, my mom always said I was special," he added in an exaggerated version of Manny speaking.

"You're just jealous," Uko replied.

"Ha! Whatever," Brandon replied as he stood up. He took two copies of the paper he'd shown them earlier with the laptop model numbers and teacher names and placed them on the table. "Just don't mess this up. This is serious."

"You got it, boss," Uko said.

After watching Manny and Adriana for a few moments, Uko looked down at the papers. Try as he might, he couldn't find any immediate clues in the random numbers. "What are you hiding, Ms. Fielder?" he said to himself as he tucked his copy away. He folded up Manny's and brought it over to him as he walked toward the cafeteria exit.

"I don't listen to rap like that," Adriana said. "I'm more into old school R&B. Real old school stuff, like from the '90s."

"That's cool," Manny replied. "My mom listens to that sometimes. Like Boyz II Men, right?"

"Yeah," Adriana laughed. "I love them."

"All right, bro, I'll talk to you later," Uko interrupted as he got to them. When Manny shook Uko's outstretched hand, Uko secretly passed him the folded-up paper from Brandon.

"Hi, Uko, nice to see you," Adriana said.

"Oh, hey. Nice to see you too," Uko replied as he walked out. As he left, he looked back at the expression on Manny's face as he and Adriana exchanged jokes. It was a bitter reminder of what it felt like to spend time with Toni.

Later that day, Uko sat in the back of Mr. Kittles' class and daydreamed about his time in Pangea. He scribbled drawings of what he remembered the Oracle's apartment looking like. He wrote down her speech to everyone in that hall the best he could. He even tried to make a sketch of the mysterious mermaid. His mind was occupied the entire class, so his body shook when Mr. Kittles loudly called his name.

"Uko, can you tell us about what makes a great leader?" he asked.

"A great leader?" Uko asked in reply to buy himself time to think.

"Yes," Mr. Kittles said. "We've been speaking about Kofi Annan from Ghana being a great leader in the United Nations. What do you think were the attributes that made him great?"

"Um," Uko started. His mind quickly tried to relay the vague information he had. "He was really well respected. People liked being around him. He worked hard to make sure people were treated fairly." He figured he couldn't be wrong with those general answers.

"Yeah, but a lot of people have those qualities. That makes you good," Mr. Kittles replied. "What do you think made him great?"

The class murmured in consideration and looked back to Uko for his response.

"I'm not sure."

Mr. Kittles smiled. "If we're all doing a group project for school together, and I'm the leader of the group, and I tell everyone what to do so that I don't have anything to do myself, would you guys like that?"

"No," the class replied.

"And if one of you were in my group and something went wrong and you needed help, but I never offered to help," he continued, "would you be happy?"

"No," the class replied again.

"Why is that?" Mr. Kittles asked everyone.

A tall boy, who always sat up front and never took off his bookbag, raised his hand to answer. "Because you're not doing nothing. You're making us do all the work."

"You're right. I'm not doing anything!" Mr. Kittles shouted back in excitement. "I'm just telling you what to do. That's what a boss does, not a leader. Nothing is done well if everyone isn't working together. If I want to lead, I gotta get my hands dirty and do the hard work too. It's like the lyrics from that song, I gotta 'get it out the mud.'"

"Get it out the mud!" another girl echoed. The class collectively laughed.

"That's right. Y'all thought I just read history books all day?" Mr. Kittles replied as the class quieted down. "A great leader is also a servant. They lead from the back of the group. And when there's hard work to be done, they get it out the mud. That's what made Kofi Annan great. He put the work in. Does that make sense, Uko?"

"Yes," Uko replied.

The class bell rang, and the students began quickly filing out.

"Homework for tomorrow are the questions at the end of Chapter 8, everyone!" Mr. Kittles called out to the class. "Uko, can you come here before you go?"

Uko gathered his things while trying to think of why he was getting in trouble. By the time he got to Mr. Kittles' desk, he hadn't come up with any answers.

"How you holdin' up?" Mr. Kittles asked him.

"I'm doing all right," Uko replied, surprised by the question.

"See ya, Mr. K," multiple students said as they left. Mr. Kittles smiled and waved back.

"You run into Simms outside of this class?" Mr. Kittles asked. "He better not be bothering you."

"No, I haven't seen him. I've been pretty much trying to lay low."

"I'm not saying to go looking for trouble, but you don't need to run and hide all day either. You got as much a right to be here as he does. Walk around with your head up."

As Mr. Kittles spoke, Principal Walker's voice boomed from the loudspeaker.

"Teachers, as a reminder, please keep your laptops on and connected to WiFi at all times. It is the only way the I.T. team can continue to send important updates."

The announcement reminded Uko of the Last Word assignment and made him look at the open laptop on Mr. Kittles' desk.

"How's that notebook you took the other day?" Mr. Kittles asked. "You get a chance to read it?"

"Oh yeah, I read the whole thing. It's really interesting."

"Really? The whole thing, huh? So what is it, someone's diary or something?"

"No, it's actually interviews that someone wrote down," Uko said without thinking. Being in his own head about Pangea for so long made him forget that it made sense to no one else. He closed his eyes when the words left his mouth.

"Interviews?" Mr. Kittles replied.

"I liked the lesson today about leadership," Uko quickly said to change subject.

Mr. Kittles stared at him for a moment before responding. Uko couldn't meet his gaze. "I'm glad you liked it. That's a life lesson that'll come in handy. No shortcuts."

"Yeah, I guess kids are always looking for shortcuts."

"Adults too. We're not special. I work with adults who are still looking for shortcuts."

Uko's eyebrows raised. "Like teachers here?"

Mr. Kittles laughed and pretended to look over his shoulder. "I've said too much."

Uko chuckled.

"Everywhere you go, there are people looking for the easy way out. This place isn't any different," Mr. Kittles replied. "Any interesting dreams lately?"

"Dreams?"

"Yeah, dreams. You didn't fall asleep in class today, so I'm wondering if you got your good dreaming out of the way before you came to school."

Uko thought about Nasir and the Oracle. "I had this dream where I met this wise old lady but she already knew about me. And she could see the future or something like that. And we talked about how she knew all these different people. Kinda weird, I know," Uko finished, feeling silly for bringing it up.

Mr. Kittles' face remained neutral and without judgment. "What did she look like?"

"She was Black—well, I think she was black. She had long wavy hair with a streak of silver in it. I don't remember what she had on."

"That's pretty interesting."

"I guess."

"What else happened?"

The alarm rang to start the next class. Uko looked at the time and panicked.

"Oh, I'm sorry," Mr. Kittles said as he searched his desk. He grabbed a Post-It note and scribbled on it. "Give this to your teacher so you don't get in trouble for being late. I'll see you in class next week. Don't forget to do the homework."

"Thanks, Mr. K," Uko replied. He put the note in his pocket and jogged out. As he went down the hall, he noticed that every three or four lockers had a picture of Manny on them. He stopped at one to read the paper.

VOTE 4 MANNY

THE 6TH GRADE CLASS PRESIDENT WE DESERVE

"Wow. Look at my guy," Uko said to himself. "No games were played. Guess we're really running for class prez."

He pulled out his phone and took a picture of the poster. Now he'd have the evidence of the campaign and Manny's goofy smile in case Manny decided to take them all down.

The school day ended without Uko getting any more info on his target, Ms. Fielder. He knew it would be tough doing surveillance on a teacher he never had class with, and today was a perfect example of why. The closest he got was staring at her in the teacher's lounge when the door was left open as he walked by. The only intel that gave him was that she liked eating baby carrots while looking at her phone. He'd need to figure out some other plan to get useful information, or he'd have to give up on trying. You can only be the weirdo staring into rooms of teachers for so long. There had to be a better way.

When he remembered that Coding Club was scheduled to meet after school today, he decided he'd bring it up to Brandon and Manny. Maybe he'd be able to have some other assignment that didn't require him stalking people. After the final school bell rang and the hallways were filled with kids joyously leaving for the day, he headed to the computer lab in the basement for the start of Coding Club. When he got there, Brandon and Manny were already standing by the door with the rest of the kids waiting for Ms. Powalski to let them in.

"What's up?" Uko said before Manny raised his hand to stop him from speaking.

"Before you say anything else," Manny started, "it was completely Adriana's idea to make the class president posters. She said it's important to start campaigning early."

Uko didn't reply. He just nodded and grinned. He looked over at Brandon and saw he was doing the same.

"I don't need this from y'all. It's tough enough to put yourself out there like this," Manny went on. He waited for either of them to reply, but they just grinned. "What? Is this about the picture? Adriana said it looked good."

"Do you think it looked good?" Uko said while pretending to sound like a concerned therapist.

"Do I?" Manny responded. "Shut up. I know what you're doing. It was my decision too."

"As long as you feel empowered," Brandon added with a soft pat on Manny's shoulder.

Manny brushed his hand off his shoulder, and the boys finally let out a laugh.

"Can you be quiet?" one of the other students said.

Before the boys could reply, Ms. Kowalski came barreling down the hall with her usual look of annoyance. Next to her was one of the women from the IT team. Without saying hello or apologizing for being late, Ms. Kowalski pulled out her keys and opened the door to the computer lab. She flicked on the lights and put her bag down by the door.

"All right, you know where to sit," Ms. Kowalski said. "New kids in the back. The rest of you sit in these two rows up here."

"Which computer are you setting it up on?" the lady from IT asked Ms. Kowalski. Without replying, she pointed to a computer in the second row. The lady sat down and began logging in.

Instead of following Manny and Uko's lead and walking to the back of the room, Brandon kept his eyes on the computers up front that had been kept off limits since he started this mission.

"Ms. Kowalski. Can we sit up front here too?" he said while waving his arms to include Uko and Manny as well. "We've watched the videos and it's cold back there. We want to be a part of the group too."

"No, you guys sit in the back," Ms. Kowalski replied. "I'll find other videos for you."

"I just don't understand why we have to be segregated," Brandon said louder as he stared at the IT woman as she worked. She turned toward him and Ms. Kowalski with a surprised look. It was enough for Brandon to keep up the pressure. "I just want to feel like I belong. My friends here don't know words yet, so they're not going to say anything."

Even now, he has to have jokes, Uko thought.

"No one is segregating," Ms. Kowalski cut in while nervously staring at the IT woman. "Just sit up here." She pointed to the row of computers right behind the group of students that she normally kept separate from the boys.

"Thank you, ma'am," Brandon added while fighting back a cheesy grin. "We promise to be the best coders that ever coded in the Coding—"

"Just sit down!" Ms. Kowalski snapped before walking away.

Brandon looked back at Uko and Manny and waved them up to their new seats in the third row, right next to the action. They all sat quietly and cheered to themselves. Brandon sat directly behind the IT woman and began looking over to spy on what she was doing.

"She's installing something," Brandon whispered to the other two.

"Can you tell what it is?" Manny whispered back.

"No, but I'll see if I can figure it out," Brandon replied. "You two open up something to take notes. We gotta take notes on everything."

The boys began getting ready with excited intensity. *Even if this ends up being nothing more than a wild goose chase*, Uko thought, *it's a fun one.* As they logged in, Brandon passed over his notebook, open to a page with tons of scribbled thoughts.

"You gotta take notes like these," he said. "This is what I got on my surveillance for the day."

As Manny and Uko bent over Brandon's notebook and tried to read the scribbles, the door to the computer lab opened.

"Your handwriting is terrible," Uko whispered to Brandon as he read.

"Hi, Ms. Kowalski," a voice said from the now opened door. The boys were too focused to look up.

"When you're doing detective work, you don't have time for perfect penmanship," Brandon shot back.

"Our teacher sent us here for the afternoon. Said we should join," the voice continued. "My name's Charles, but everyone calls me Simms."

Uko dropped the notebook as he turned to the door in shock. His mind couldn't accept what his eyes were telling him. There in the doorway stood Simms and two other guys who were both somehow even bigger.

"Are you kidding me?" Ms. Kowalski muttered. "This isn't a halfway house."

Simms ignored her. After scanning the room when he first walked in, his eyes were now focused solely on Uko. He pointed to the row of seats directly behind Uko, Brandon, and Manny.

"Can we sit there?"

"Sure," Ms. Kowalski replied. "Do whatever you want."

CHAPTER 18

Gumshoe Detective

"What? What is it? Why do you look like you just saw a ghost?" Brandon whispered to Uko.

Uko looked at the door and realized what was going on. He didn't know what to do. Should he just run now and ignore the embarrassment of looking like a crazy person in the lab? Would they chase him? If he stayed, would they attack him right here in front of everyone else? Simms and company sauntered over to the seats behind the boys, with Simms happily taking the seat directly behind Uko.

"Do you have a pen I can use?" Simms leaned forward and said to Uko.

"I don't think you need a pen, bro. You're probably just gonna be watching a lot of videos," Brandon replied.

"Shut up," Simms replied. "I wasn't talking to you, Baby B." Simms and the other boys laughed.

"Wow, you remember that?" one boy said to Simms.

"Quiet!" Ms. Kowalski yelled from the front. "If you're going to be here, you have to lower your voices. We're working."

"What's everyone working on, Ms. Kowalski?" Simms defiantly asked.

Uko leaned over to Brandon, who now seemed to be in a bad mood. "I gotta go," Uko whispered.

"We're working on coding, Mr. Simms," Ms. Kowalski replied. "Since you and your friends are new, you'll be watching some videos to get started."

"What do you mean you gotta go?" Brandon replied. His anger from Simms' comment pushed the volume of his words higher than their previous whispers. The repetition of the words was embarrassing for Uko to hear. He didn't need reinforcement of his decision to run from his problems.

"You gotta go?" Simms immediately jumped in after overhearing. "We just got here. Where you going?"

"All set, Ms. Kowalski," the IT woman said suddenly. "The program is here, and it'll work on your laptop in a few minutes as well." She got up and started collecting her things. The computer and the program that the boys were hoping to get a sneak peak of were now closing and turning off.

"Thank you, Mary," Ms. Kowalski replied. She stood up and began walking toward her.

Uko looked over at Manny. Without saying anything, Manny nodded. Uko turned to Brandon and leaned closer. "I'll explain later. But I have to go now. If you want to come, you're gonna have to run."

Brandon was silent for a few seconds before sneaking a glance at Simms and his friends. He nodded and turned his chair toward the row behind them.

"Matter fact, I do have a pen you can use," Brandon said while setting his open water bottle on the table in front of Simms. With his other hand, he placed his bookbag on the floor between them and then bent down to pull something out of it.

Uko slowly grabbed his bookbag and pushed his chair back just enough to give him space to run. He just needed the right moment to escape. Manny, the closest to the door, did the same. As they did, Mary from IT and Ms. Kowalski both reached the door. Mary began explaining something to Ms. Kowalksi before exiting.

"There it is," Brandon said as he pulled a pen out of his bookbag quickly. In the process, he knocked over his water bottle with his arm so that it spilled onto their table. He leaned onto the water bottle with his forearm and pressed it down. The water shot out like a small fire hydrant into Simms' face.

"What are you doing?!" Simms screamed as he covered his eyes.

"Hey!" Ms. Kowalski yelled from the door. Mary from IT turned to see what the commotion was about.

Both Manny and Uko shot up and ran for the door. In perfect unison, they squeezed behind Ms. Kowalski, opened the lab's door, and darted out.

As they left, Simms tapped his friend's arm, and they began chasing them. Halfway down the hall, Uko turned back to see Ms. Kowalski and the IT woman act as a barrier for Simms and his friends. They had to work their way around the women, buying Uko and Manny the head start they needed.

The boys charged out of the school and ran down the street as fast as they could. After a few minutes they looked back to see if Simms and company were close. When they realized they weren't, they stopped and tried to catch their breath. After a few seconds of leaning over and gasping for air, they crumpled to the ground in laughter. People stared at the weird kids sitting in the middle of the sidewalk looking hysterical. They didn't care. They'd gotten away.

"I can't believe that happened," Manny said between laughs.

"I know," Uko replied. "I know."

The boys got back on their feet and proceeded to finish their walk home. They replayed the craziness of the afternoon as they breezed through the city streets, exchanging stories and bluffs about what they would have done if they'd had to stay and confront Simms.

As they walked onto their block, Manny spotted his brother Carlos getting out of the family car with his mom and dad. "They just picked up Carlos. They're gonna wonder why I'm home so early," Manny said.

"Tell them Coding Club ended early," Uko replied.

"You think they're gonna believe that?"

"No, probably not," Uko laughed.

"You're so helpful for all things needed in my life."

"It's tiring, but I do the best I can."

"Wow. Look at the sacrifice. You deserve a Nobel Peace Prize."

"I do. I really do," Uko replied while searching his bookbag for his keys. "But seriously, you know I got you, right?"

"Always."

"And I know I was messing with you before, but if you wanna run for class president, just let me know what help you need from me."

"Cool. Remember you said that," Manny replied. "Adriana has all these plans, and I need help with a lot of it."

"If it's too much, I can still decide I don't want to do it."

"Nope, that's not how this works. I saved your life today so now you're locked in."

"That's fair."

The boys said their goodbyes, and Uko went into his unusually quiet home. He took advantage of being home first and headed to his room in peace. He dropped his bags, said 'what's up' to Kanju, and collapsed onto his bed. Running for his life, even for a few minutes, had worked up an insane appetite for dinner. It wasn't enough to get him to actually make something himself, but it was enough for his stomach to count the seconds until the rest of the family got home.

Later that night after dinner was eaten, showers were taken, teeth were brushed, video games were played, and homework was finished, Uko laid in bed and thought through the day. He didn't know how, but he knew that at some point he would have to find a solution for his Simms problem. He'd rather not involve teachers and make it into a super big deal, but he thought he might need to at least tell Mr. K. He told Uko's dad that he'd look out for him. This would be something he'd want to know.

Speaking of Mr. Kittles, Uko thought. *Get it out the mud.*

He chuckled to himself and drifted off to sleep. No matter how crazy life had gotten in middle school, at least he was familiar with Pangea.

❖ ❖ ❖

"What's up, Commander?" Nasir said coolly.

Uko's eyes shot around as he tried to figure out what was happening. After a few seconds, his racing mind settled. He was back in his dream limbo, the supernaturally quiet meadow with tall grass and perfect temperatures. He was sitting on one of the large logs that circled an extinguished campfire on the edge of the field. There were butterflies gracefully dancing in and out of sight, and the sun was setting the same way it always did. The only major difference was his newly acquired right-hand man Nasir was sitting on a log across from him with his legs crossed. He got up and brushed his pants in anticipation.

"How did you get here?" Uko asked.

"We're connected, bro," Nasir replied. "I'm here 'cause we got work to do. You don't get the Oracle's blessing and then sit on your butt. It's action time."

Uko got up from the log and began following Nasir as he turned toward the forest and Uko's Silk Road.

"We got work to do?" Uko repeated.

"If we're gonna find and then eventually destroy Chief, you're gonna need a crew," Nasir replied. "We need one that's above ground and another one that's underground. The above ground crew is the one that all of Pangea, including Chief, knows about. That group has gotta be big enough and serious enough to get his attention and keep it. At the same time, you need another crew of people doing stuff behind the scenes. In the shadows. They don't claim you. They act like they got no beef with Chief or the Coyotes. But that underground crew might be more important than anyone else."

"What does the underground crew do?"

"They're the spies. They're the ones giving us intelligence about everything. If they get a chance and they're good at what they do, they're sabotaging Chief without him even knowing it. The Cuckoo birds." The boys began their walk toward the forest. "In real life, a Cuckoo bird lays its eggs in the nest of another bird. The Cuckoo eggs hatch faster and grow faster than the other birds in the nest. By the time the host bird realizes it's been raising some foreign bird, it's too late."

"Dope. How do we get them?"

186

"I'll help you with the aboveground crew. I'll introduce you to some people who can help too. But that will be your mission. I'll handle the underground group by myself."

"I can't do both?"

"It ain't much of a secret crew if the leader is assembling it himself," Nasir replied. He walked so quickly that Uko practically had to jog to keep up. "If you got anyone special you want me to recruit, let me know."

"Seriously?" Uko said as his thoughts immediately centered on one person.

"Yeah," Nasir said. When he saw the expression on Uko's face, he stopped for the first time in their conversation. "Who you got in mind?"

"There's this girl who recruited me for the Nightmare Detectives. She was retiring, so she's not a Detective anymore. But she's really good. Her name's Toni. We did a lot together," Uko replied. He thought fondly about the time they spent and how incredible it would be to see her again.

"When was the last time you connected with her?"

"It's been a minute. I haven't seen her since she retired and passed the torch to me. I know we're not supposed to stay in contact after that, but if we're doing something like this, maybe we can make an exception."

Nasir nodded his head slowly. "I'll check out your DreamHub. If you two had a strong connection, I should be able to find her."

"Yeah, we did."

"You want her with the secret forces or out in the open?"

"Either one is fine."

"I'll see what I can do," Nasir replied. "You must have really liked her."

Uko stared at his feet. "I mean, yeah. She's cool. She would really be great in the crew."

"Really liked her," Nasir repeated and smirked.

"Do you need anything else?" Uko quickly asked.

"Let's give it a name. So when we're building up the team, we can call ourselves something," Nasir replied. "You're already part of the Nightmare Detectives crew, so you can just recruit people to join that. People know about them already, so it'll be easier to get the word around so Chief hears about it."

"But I don't lead the Nightmare Detectives," Uko replied. "I can't just recruit a bunch of people to join. I'm supposed to find my replacement when I'm done, but that's it."

"Nobody runs it. Y'all are just operating on your own. You might link up from time to time, but it's not like you have meetings or something. There was a little structure when it was first started, but it's not like that anymore."

"And I'm supposed to become the new leader of the Nightmare Detectives? Bring all these kids together by myself? Are you crazy?" Uko replied.

"That's exactly what you're gonna do. And you're going to recruit adults too. You may not realize it, but getting the blessing from the Oracle is a big freakin' deal. All those people in the hall that night, those were heavy hitters. They didn't say they were down just so you can do this thing halfway. Chief has been a bigger problem for Pangea than you know. If the Oracle says you're gonna lead the fight, then this is what it looks like."

Uko recalled the faces of those people in the hallway, the conviction in their pledges. Expectation weighs a ton.

"You think that's possible?"

"I know it is. And it'll come from you. Whatever needs to happen will come together. I'm confident in that," Nasir replied. They reached the edge of the forest and the beginning of the Silk Road to Uko's DreamHub. Nasir stepped onto the path and began walking without looking back. Uko followed.

"Okay then," Uko finally said as he gathered his thoughts. "I'll do it."

"You make it sound like you had a choice," Nasir replied. "You were built for this."

The path was quickly growing darker as they went deeper into the forest. Nasir easily navigated the rocks and logs along the way as he led.

"What are we gonna call the underground crew?" Uko asked.

"You think it needs a name?"

"Yeah, even spies have names. Like the CIA," Uko replied.

"True. You got something in mind?" Nasir asked. "Ouch!"

Uko looked over, but it was now too dark to see Nasir. "What happened?"

"Hit my head on a branch."

"Aren't I supposed to be leading you and not the other way around? This is my Silk Road, ain't it?" Uko asked. "I'm the one who knows all the twists and turns with my eyes closed."

"Yeah. I just wanted to see if I could figure it out," Nasir replied. "Take the lead, Commander."

"You really gonna keep calling me that?"

"I think it's funny," Nasir replied. "Or, it's funny now, but one day people will be calling you Commander for real. Get used to it."

"Whatever."

As they entered the center of the forest, the all too familiar plume of silver and purple fog billowed down in front of them. The cloudy images of faces laughing, screaming and crying swirled in and out of focus. Now that Uko could see Nasir again, he watched him examine the fog like a doctor reading an X-ray.

Finally, Nasir spoke. "You got a name for my crew?"

"Huh?"

"My underground CIA gang of misfits and Cuckoo birds," Nasir replied. "What are we gonna be called?"

Uko thought for a moment before a childhood memory popped in his head.

"There was this cartoon I used to watch about a dog that solved complex crimes that no one else could figure out," Uko said. "Everybody called him a Gumshoe because he was better than everybody on the police force."

"What's a Gumshoe?"

"I don't really know, but it sounds cool," Uko replied.

Nasir quietly laughed. "So that's what we're going with? Gumshoes?" he asked.

Uko thought about it. "Gumshoe Detectives."

"Gumshoe Detectives?"

"Yeah. We'll have Nightmare Detectives doing everything in the open and then we'll have Gumshoe Detectives in the shadows."

"Gumshoe Detectives," Nasir repeated. He looked back at the DreamHub and stared at the spiraling images as they danced in the mist. "I can work with that."

CHAPTER 19

New Recruits

"I have somewhere to take you," Nasir said as he pointed at a syrupy blotch in the fog. Uko moved to inspect it but Nasir wouldn't let him. "Just tap it and let's go," he barked. Uko obliged.

BANG

Uko blinked slowly as his vision came back. He was seated in a cramped booth in what looked like a busy diner. Nasir sat across from him with a massive menu open as he read it.

"Where is this?" Uko asked.

Nasir looked up at him before taking a sip from a mug of coffee in front of him. "Rosewood Diner," he replied as he smacked his lips. "Pangea crowd favorite."

A waiter walked over to the two of them and pulled out a small notepad. As he searched for his pen, Nasir raised his hand to stop him.

"We're not gonna be eating anything. We came to get some gas," Nasir said. The waiter looked more closely at Uko and Nasir and put his notepad away.

"Have you two been fishing here before?" the waiter asked.

Uko squinted his eyes as he tried to keep up with what was being said.

"I've never been here," Nasir said before pointing at Uko across from him. "But he's a regular."

The waiter looked over at Uko. "What's your name?"

Uko looked at Nasir for assistance in case this was another riddle.

"You don't know your name?" Nasir asked.

"It's Uko."

The waiter nodded and then walked through a set of double doors into the kitchen.

"What was that?" Uko whispered. He felt like he was in the middle of a spy movie.

"You'll see," Nasir said as he slid over in his booth seat toward the window. He made room as if he were expecting company, then pointed to the spot near the window. "Move over."

Uko cautiously slid over, and just as he did, a woman appeared out of nowhere, closed a large umbrella dripping with water, and sat down next to Nasir. Uko looked from the woman to Nasir and back to the woman but neither acknowledged the other's presence. They both just stared at Uko. After a second of awkward silence, a burly man slid in next to Uko while a boy that looked to be Uko's age sat next to the woman on Nasir's side of the booth.

"Can we help you?" Uko asked with little authority. No one answered. They either looked around the diner or focused their attention on Uko. Before he could ask a follow-up question, the diner's kitchen doors swung open and an older woman in a chef's uniform stepped out with the waiter behind her. The waiter scanned the diner before pointing at Uko. The chef briskly walked over to the table and sat in the last empty space on his side. Uko opened his mouth to speak before being cut off by Nasir.

"Thanks for coming. The Oracle would appreciate the solidarity."

"I don't think it's a good idea to gather in such a public place," the boy said softly.
With an expressive tilting of his head, Nasir scanned the diner. "I'm not worried about nobody here. The Oracle wants us to ride, we ride. Right, Uko?"

Uko felt the jolt that happens when a teacher calls your name in a class you were not paying attention to. "What do you mean?"

"Where are my manners?" Nasir said. He pointed to each member of the table as he introduced them. "This lovely lady next to me is Mel, this brute sitting next to you is Bronson, that's Christopher at the end there, and of course the last member is Chef Flores. These are your first recruits."

Uko scanned the hodgepodge table. It wasn't even three months ago when he was learning the rules of being a Nightmare Detective and the pledge to retire when you reached high school. Now here he was with one kid his age and a bunch of adults who were supposed to be new Detectives.

"They're going to be Nightmare Detectives?" Uko asked. "I think they're too old. No offense," he added to the group. Chef Flores smiled.

"Things are different now, Uko. I told you it was gonna have to change if you plan on taking down the Coyotes," Nasir replied. "You need reinforcements from some Pangea vets."

As Nasir spoke, the diner customers that walked past their table continued to look at the group. Uko noticed the hushed whispers and curious eyes of the people all around them.

"Bronson's the best shapeshifter I know, Mel has vision, Christopher is a Nightmare Detective like you, and Chef Flores' specialty is pace," Nasir added.

Uko looked at each person as they stared back at him. "What are all those things? What's pace, Ms. Flores?" he finally asked.

"Chef Flores," she replied. "I worked hard to get that title."

"Sorry. Chef Flores," Uko replied.

"Like I said," Nasir continued. "You need different skills, and you need a bunch of people who can do them. Pace is the speed of a dream or nightmare. Chef Flores can speed things up or slow them down, even when she's in someone else's dream. Not easily done and extremely clutch. We used it when we went to meet the Oracle. A shapeshifter is what it sounds like. Bronson can change into different things when needed. And when I say Mel has vision, I mean she can see what's coming next. Not all the time, and not that far in the future. But just enough," Nasir replied. "Everyone in Pangea has the ability to do these things, we're just not that great at it. These are the experts."

Uko looked over at the only other boy at the table--Christopher. "And he's a Nightmare Detective like me."

"He's better than you," Nasir quickly replied.

Uko's head snapped back. "What do you mean he's better?" he asked defensively. Christopher smirked.

"How many nightmares do you think you've solved since you became a Detective?" Nasir asked.

"I don't know. I'm not keeping track like it's a game or something. I know it's been more than a hundred," Uko replied, knowing that he had been keeping track and he'd done seventy-three.

"I've done 437," Christopher casually stated. "I'm just saying it."

"You guys started at the same time," Nasir added.

Uko used all his energy to avoid looking surprised. "Some of us can't be asleep our entire lives. We have things to do."

The entire table, including Christopher, laughed. Uko felt a flash of frustration for a moment before nearly crumpling under the heavy pat of Bronson's hand on his shoulder.

"You're funny, kid," Bronson said as he used his other hand to wipe tears from his eyes.

"Nothing to worry about, Uko," Mel said. "It's not a competition. We all report to you. We want the same thing that you do."

Uko looked around the table again. The faces were indeed all welcoming. Even the overachiever Christopher. His hurt pride simmered down and was replaced by the sensation of being out of his comfort zone.

"Okay then. What do we do now?" Uko asked. "The last time I saw Chief, he lured me into a trap and killed me. I have no idea how to find him now."

"What was he like?" Christopher asked with wonder.

Uko could practically feel the growl of Chief's voice as he remembered being attacked in that school gym. "He's intense."

"You're a brave young man," Chef Flores said. "I've never seen anyone make it their mission to challenge him."

"Sounds like a suicide mission to me," Bronson interrupted. "You love to see it."

"Have any of you ever seen him?" Uko asked the group. No one met his eye. Finally, Nasir spoke up.

"Everyone here has been affected by him in some way. That's why they agreed to help you when I reached out to them."

"Chief is the reason I'm not with my brother right now," Bronson cut in. His eyes stared at the table as he spoke. "He's in a high security psych hospital for hurting this couple and then saying that voices made him do it. He wasn't lying. It was Chief and two of his Coyotes visiting him every night for fun. They wanted to see if they could make someone lose their mind. It worked."

The table fell silent after Bronson spoke. He rubbed his eyes and looked back up at Uko. "You can say I'm a little motivated."

"I don't have some master plan to get rid of him. I just know that this can't keep going on," Uko said.

"We don't need a superhero," Chef Flores replied. "We need someone who can be in the middle of the fight with us. If we all do what we can, we might do something miraculous."

The hope in everyone's tone gave Uko courage he hadn't known he needed. Slowly, it felt more and more real. "How do we start?"

"Great question," Nasir replied as he gestured for the rest of the people in his row to slide out. As they did, he scooted over to the end of the booth and got to his feet. He looked over to Chef Flores, who was already rising in anticipation.

"Chef, I need you to quit this job. Publicly," Nasir said. "The diner's full enough now to get the amount of attention I was hoping for. It'll be a sort of press release for us."

Chef Flores smiled and looked at the double doors she'd come through. As if her gaze had the power to summon, the waiter that first escorted her to the table came from out of the kitchen. He was quickly followed by another man in a chef's uniform similar to hers. Neither of them looked pleased.

"Chef," the waiter said in a heightened whisper as he looked the group over. "Things are backed up. We need your help back in the kitchen."

The other cook cut into the conversation. "I don't know what reunion you have going on, but we gotta get back to work." He was much more agitated.

Chef Flores turned to the waiter and chef and responded much more loudly than would normally be necessary. "I quit, guys. I'm not going back."

"What?" the cook replied. He was now so frustrated he pushed Nasir aside and stepped directly in front of Chef Flores. "Are you kidding? This better not be some stupid joke."

"No, it's not a joke," Chef Flores calmly replied. Uko noticed that the previous buzz of the diner was replaced with attentive silence. This exchange was the most important thing happening in the building right now. Several phones were raised in the air as their owners recorded the altercation. "I'm done with this." She dramatically took off her chef's hat and tossed it on the booth's table. She then unbuttoned her white coat and placed that down as well, exposing the rolled-up sleeves and forearm tattoos that her uniform normally hid.

"Let's head out," Nasir said.

The now irate cook turned on him with a look of malice in his eyes. But before he could do anything, Bronson's meaty palm grabbed his shoulder. "No, no, no, buddy," Bronson said. "I think you should just get back to what you were doing."

The chef turned to Bronson and deflated when he noticed how big he was. "Whatever," he huffed before storming back into the kitchen. The waiter picked up Chef Flores' uniform and followed him. The dozens of eyes in the diner and the multitude of cell phones didn't miss a second.

"That went well," Mel chuckled. Uko was at a loss for words.

"Let's go," Nasir said before turning towards the exit. The group left the diner and its hungry audience. As Uko walked out, he snuck a glance at the kitchen through a narrow window where waiters picked up food orders. All the cooks stared back in shock as the group walked out.

"Where do you live?" Christopher asked Uko as they left.

"Newark. What about you?"

"Atlanta."

"Cool."

"By the way, that whole thing about who's done more nightmares—I wasn't trying to show off or anything," Christopher said. "I don't want you to feel a way about that. We should start off on the right foot. You know what I mean?"

Uko nodded. "Yeah, I'm good. I think it's dope that you've done that many. You gotta show me your secrets."

Christopher grinned. "No, you gotta tell me about what it was like to meet the Oracle. That's wild."

Nasir led the group as they crossed the street and walked down a busy block full of people. The newly minted Detectives held conversations among themselves in pairs as they followed Nasir's lead. Uko could hear Mel's funny imitations of everyone's voices as she retold Chef Flores' quitting story to Bronson. His belly laughs were so full and contagious, it was hard to imagine him as anything but a silly giant. One with hands the size of baseball mitts.

"The Oracle was incredible. She, like, questioned me on my feelings about Chief and the Coyotes while she taught me how to play spades," Uko replied to Christopher.

"She taught you how to play spades too!?" he gushed. "That's an even better story."

Uko's chest swelled with pride. It *was* a great story.

"Christopher, I need another DreamHub," Nasir cut in from the front of the pack. He pointed down an alley they had just reached. Uko glanced down the vacant path as he and Christopher caught up to the rest of the pack. There was an overfilled dumpster, some scattered cardboard boxes, and not much else. The group stood to the side as Christopher walked toward the middle of the alley. Bright orange mist shot up from the ground in front of him like a geyser. He stared up into the fog as it climbed higher and higher, blocking any view past it. The same shadowy images that Uko would see in his own DreamHub darted back and forth through the plumes. As the group joined Christopher in front of it, Uko marveled at how clear some of the images were. He often had to interpret his poorly defined outlines the best he could when selecting a dream. Christopher's DreamHub was like a high-def video.

"This looks great," Mel commented, followed by a chorus of "I know!" from the others in the group.

"Thanks," Christopher quietly replied. "Where do you want to go?" he asked Nasir.

Nasir stared at the swirls in silence for a few moments before pointing to something to his far right.

"To Yomi," he replied. "We gotta recruit some lifers."

"Are you sure?" Bronson asked. For the first time, his voice betrayed his normally jolly demeanor. He sounded concerned.

"Yeah. We're gonna need help from the people who've spent the most time here in Pangea," Nasir replied. "From now on, there isn't any letting up. The fight will be constant. We ain't ready for that on our own."

"Okay. Let's do it then," Mel replied. She walked over to the image of what looked like people sitting up in beds and held out her hand. The fog pooled around it like foam. As the rest of the group walked to join her, Uko approached Christopher.

"What is Yomi?" he asked.

"It's a gathering place for some people who are always in Pangea because they can't wake up. They're...stuck," Christopher replied somberly. "In Pangea, they're in Yomi because in real life, they're in a coma."

CHAPTER 20

The Residents of Yomi

This time, Uko didn't experience the familiar flash of bright light that usually comes from jumping dreams. This transition was gradual and dull. The group went from being outside in an alley during the middle of the day to a poorly lit room that would benefit from fresher air. Things came into Uko's vision piece by piece—starting from an empty black space and gradually filling the canvas with objects and people. The group was a few feet in front of Uko, already in the middle of conversation with each other. No one seemed to notice his arrival. As he watched the group speak with a frail-looking man in robes, Nasir walked alongside him and startled Uko.

"How you feelin'?" he asked.

"What?! I thought you were up there with them. What's going on?"

"No. Got here just a little after you. There's usually a delay when jumping into Yomi," Nasir replied. He noticed Uko staring at the others in the group, speaking with a hunched-over old man in robes. "They're negotiating with the gatekeeper."

"That old guy?" Uko asked, pointing at the robed man holding court in the middle of the group. He moved slowly and when he spoke, his words were so soft that everyone had to lean in to hear him clearly.

"He's the only way you get into Yomi. This isn't a tourist attraction. You gotta have a good reason to be here.."

"What's our good reason?"

"We're planning to attack the Coyotes and get rid of Chief. Yomi is filled with people from every time zone in the world," Nasir replied. "If we can convince enough of the residents of Yomi to assist us, we'll have help when you're awake doing classwork in school or whatever it is you do."

"And these people are sick? They're in comas in real life?" Uko asked.

"Not everyone is sick. But something brought them here. It could be from a bad accident or some type of injury. Sometimes they get the help they need, recover, and they leave Yomi. Go back to happy lives," Nasir replied. Uko saw him raise a balled fist to his cheek to wipe a lone tear. "Sometimes they don't."

Uko looked down after Nasir spoke. He knew Nasir had some other connection to this place but couldn't think of the right way to ask. Nasir offered nothing, so they stood next to each other in silence.

"Let's go, guys," Bronson called to the two of them.

Each person in the group took a turn to shake the gatekeeper's hand. He ended each interaction with a slight bow. When Uko and Nasir walked to him, Nasir shook his hand and expressed thanks. Uko decided to follow the lead.

"Good luck to you," he said in reply. He then bowed his head lower and put his hand to his heart. Uko looked to see if anyone else had noticed. Nasir looked back at him and nodded.

"Where do we go now?" Uko asked.

"We're already here," Mel replied.

Uko looked around to see the small room they'd stood in before replaced with what looked like a warehouse floor. As far as he could see, there were rows and rows of neatly arranged cots. Each one had shabby bedding and a small pillow. At the foot of each bed was the same grayish-blue trunk. As he looked around, he saw a swarm of people walking back and forth through the open space. Some people sat on their cots, others picked through the contents in the trunks at the end of their beds, and others slept. What mesmerized Uko the most was the vast range in ages of everyone he saw. There were people older than his grandparents as well as boys and girls much younger than himself. They were all here. Stuck together, in Yomi.

As Uko continued to stare while trying to not be obvious, a strong feeling of *déjà vu* overcame him. His head jerked back as it set in.

I've been here before. When I had that daydream in Mr. K's class, he thought.

The memory came back to him swiftly. He'd fallen asleep for a brief second in class and somehow dreamed about this place. Was it something happening in the moment? Was it somehow the future? Was it the past? He wasn't sure. He remembered watching someone remove bloodstained bandages and complain about some contract they had. The room he was in now seemed infinitely larger than what he'd seen the first time. He might have been in a small section of this vast warehouse.

"Let's split up," Nasir said quietly. Everyone stood in a huddle as they discussed their next step, while the residents walked around them with suspicious eyes. Although there wasn't an identifying uniform in Yomi, Uko and the group stood out as outsiders.

"Me, Uko and Chef Flores will go speak to a few people. Bronson—you, Christopher and Mel will talk to others," Nasir added. "We don't want to turn people off by being super pushy. And we don't want to attract a big crowd. This has to be something where we speak to people one-on-one. I have a feeling we're not the first people to attempt something like this. I don't want to have people make up their minds before we've even had a personal convo."

"Got it," Bronson replied. He looked over at Christopher and Mel. Everyone nodded, and they turned toward the left side of the room and began wandering.

"Don't be nervous," Chef Flores said to Uko. It was as if she could read his mind. Or at least his body language.

"Okay," Uko replied without conviction. He followed as Nasir and Chef Flores walked up to a girl that had been staring at them from her cot since they appeared. She was young, probably around Uko's age.

"Hello," Nasir began.

"Yes?" she coldly replied.

"My name is Nasir. This is Uko, and this is Chef Flores."

"Y'all on a field trip or something? What do you want?"

"No, no, nothing like that," Chef Flores replied. "We're here on serious business."

"We need help," Uko said.

"For what?"

"Have you heard of the Coyotes?" Uko asked.

"Look, I don't need this," she said. "I'm not supposed to be here. I'm not trying to get mixed up in any of that stuff. I'm just gonna do my time until I can leave." She got up and walked away from the group. They watched her in silence, trying to figure out how well they did in their first attempt. Uko looked over to Bronson's group and saw the person they were speaking to raise their hands, shake their heads, and walk away as well.

"Never said this was gonna be easy," Nasir said.

"Ain't that the truth," Chef Flores replied.

"On to the next one," Nasir said as he approached another resident. "Hi, can I talk to you for a second?"

Uko and Chef Flores joined the conversation. The man they spoke to was tall and heavyset and looked like he would be one of Uko's father's friends. He smiled and seemed receptive.

"My name's Nasir. Can I ask what your name is?"

"Darnell."

"I don't want you to feel pestered, Darnell," Chef Flores said. "This is Uko and I'm Chef Flores."

Darnell furrowed his brow. "I've heard of you." He pointed at Chef Flores. "You run the Rosewood Diner, right?"

"That's right," Chef Flores replied. "That's me."

"What are you doing here?"

"We're trying to help this young man Uko."

Uko felt his face get warm as the conversation shifted to him.

"Have you heard of Chief and the Coyotes?" Nasir asked.

Darnell didn't immediately reply. Instead he examined Uko more closely while he unsuccessfully tried to return the eye contact.

"What type of trouble are y'all in?" Darnell finally said.

"No trouble at all," Chef Flores replied. "We're here because we plan on taking them down and we want help from the entire Pangea community. Yomi is no different. Uko here is going to lead it."

"Him?" Darnell replied with obvious shock.

"Yes, me," Uko said. He reluctantly locked eyes with Darnell.

"He's gotten the blessing from the Oracle," Nasir added. "I know you know who—"

"You're lying."

"No, we're serious," Chef Flores replied. "Hasn't happened in forever."

"Well the last time it happened, look where it got us," Darnell said. He looked Uko up and down. "I'd be careful who you tell that to. You're lucky you're speaking to me. Not everyone here would be open to hearing news about attacking the Coyotes and Chief."

"Why is that?" Uko asked.

"You think you're the first ones to come to Yomi to get people on your side? Them Coyotes got roots in here. Roots that run deep."

Chef Flores looked to the ceiling and shook her head.

"Yeah, this isn't new to us. We've seen the song and dance before," Darnell continued. "I don't get myself into all of that stuff because it's not a game. Pangea isn't the same for us."

"We know," Nasir offered.

"No, you don't," Darnell shot back. "If you're asking people to fight the Coyotes, you better understand what that means. What they're risking. The Isle of the Dead hits different when you're from Yomi. Most of us don't come back from that. Most of us never wake up. Is that what you knew?"

"No," Chef Flores softly replied.

"I thought so."

"He's leaving," Mel suddenly cut in from behind the group. Everyone turned to her in surprise as she pointed at Uko. "He's gonna wake up."

"I am?" Uko asked. He didn't feel the normal sensation that came with waking up. The room wasn't getting brighter, everyone's words didn't seem far away. He felt present.

"Vision, remember?" Mel replied before walking back toward her group.

Uko looked to Chef Flores and Nasir. "It's fine. I'll try and stay asleep. This is important."

"Never take the opportunity to wake up and leave this place for granted, young man," Darnell said. His tone was harsh, but his face seemed more forgiving.

"It's all right, Uko," Chef Flores replied. "We'll take it from here. When you're back in Pangea, we'll fill you in. Go enjoy your day."

Before Uko could say thank you or goodbye to either of them, he was suddenly awake. Without warning he was watching his bedroom ceiling fan whirl. He was awake again with more questions than answers. The only certain thing was that his time in Pangea from now on would be completely different. His life was now on a crash course with Chief's. He'd asked to be someone who made change, and now he was getting his wish.

Uko rushed through his morning routine in preparation for another day at school. As he brushed his teeth, took his shower, playfully punched Femi back after being interrupted, and said his hellos to his parents as they watched the morning news and ran around in their own routines, his mind remained in Pangea. It was too much to keep to himself. He decided that he'd bring it up to Manny. It'd been a while since he went into detail about Pangea with him. There is only so much you can say to someone about your dreams without feeling like a burden. But today was different. This deserved some discussion—preferably with the Council. It'd been long enough.

"Don't forget your bus money, Coco," Uko's mom reminded him as she planted a goodbye kiss. He realized he had forgotten, and immediately ran back up to his room to grab it. From the bottom of the stairs, Uko's dad yelled up to him and Femi.

"Boys, you're in luck. Manny and his parents are gonna give you guys a ride to school today. Hurry up before they change their minds. Your mom and I are heading out."

Perfect, Uko thought. If Manny's parents were giving everyone a ride to school, then he'd have an impromptu meeting of the Council to catch them up on what was happening. He grabbed his cell, which he'd apparently also forgotten, and typed out the text **Four in the Park** before sending it to the Council. Might as well make it official.

After Femi's phone in the next room binged with the announcement of a new text, Uko heard him yell out, "You're so annoying!"

Uko ignored him and packed his bag before running downstairs.

Carlos opened the sliding door to the Morales family car to let him in. Uko said hello to everyone and thanked Manny's parents for the ride before crawling into the back seat between Manny and Carlos. After Femi joined them, the door slid shut, and the group was on their way.

"You called a Four in the Park, my guy?" Carlos turned around in his seat as they pulled away.

"He's doing too much, that's what it is," Femi replied and rolled his eyes.

"Ignore him," Uko replied. "I actually wanted to talk to everyone. You guys dropping us off worked out perfectly."

Manny turned in his seat with a look of concern. "What happened?"

"It's about Pangea," Uko replied.

"Son!" Carlos replied with exasperation before turning back around.

"Come on now," Femi replied as he threw his hands in the air.

"Listen, I get it. You're tired of hearing about it. You think I would bring this up if it wasn't big?" Uko replied. "I haven't even talked to you guys about it for months."

"Okay, tell us what it is," Manny said.

Uko took a deep breath before speaking. It was hard to open up and be honest—especially when the people you're talking to don't experience your issues the same way you do. But Uko decided to push forward anyway. He'd rather be vulnerable and supported than closed off while trying to figure it out himself.

"I think I got myself in too deep. You know how I've been trying to get rid of that guy Chief ever since I found out about him?" Uko said. The boys nodded. "It's just been a thought before. Something that would be nice if it happened.

But now it's different. I put myself in this spot where it's real and it's up to me to go through with it."

"What do you mean?" Femi asked. Everyone seemed more interested now.

"I met some people in Pangea. And they introduced me to other people. And everyone agrees that we gotta get rid of Chief. But they put me in charge," Uko continued. His voice was a little shaky. "This guy Nasir introduced me to the Oracle. She's this old lady who everyone knows and respects. And she told everyone that she wants me to be the one to lead the fight against Chief."

"What about that girl?" Carlos asked. "The one you met first and taught you about all of this. What did she say?"

"I haven't seen her in a minute," Uko regretfully answered. The car went silent before Manny's mom cut in.

"We're here, Carlito. Get your stuff together," she said.

"That sucks," Manny replied. "So it's just you against this guy?"

"No, it's gonna be a big group of people. Almost like an army or something, and I'm supposed to lead 'em."

"Cool, so you got a squad," Carlos said.

"Yeah, but I ain't a leader."

"Yes you are. You just don't believe it yet," Femi replied.

"See yourself the way the Oracle sees you," Manny added.

"So y'all would let me be your leader?"

"Find us in Pangea and we'll ride," Carlos replied as he exited the car. "You can't be that bad."

CHAPTER 21

Teacher Lounge Secrets

After Carlos left, the conversation was dominated by Manny's parents. Against Manny's wishes, they asked Femi and Uko about school, their parents, and everything else they wanted to catch up on. By the time there was a long enough break in the questions for Manny and Uko to talk to each other, they were already in front of their school.

"Make sure you tell your parents to come over this weekend for dinner," Manny's dad called to them as they left.

"Okay, Mr. Morales," Uko replied as he slung his bookbag on and closed the door. Before they could take more than a few steps toward the school, Brandon appeared out of nowhere and approached them.

"Well, if it ain't the Olympic track team," he said.

"What?" Uko replied.

"I know you didn't forget," Brandon said. "Ya'll booked it out of that computer lab like your lives depended on it."

"Ohhhh," Uko said, finally remembering his incident with Simms the day before. He had been so focused on his time in Pangea, he forgot about narrowly escaping Simms. The reminder didn't sit well with Uko. He would have preferred to stand up for himself. He knew he would never fight Simms, but he could have brought attention to what was happening and gotten help from Ms. Kowalski or another adult. Running away didn't solve anything. It just pushed the problem to a different day.

"Of course, a master of deception like myself had to create a diversion," Brandon continued. "But I gotta admit that you guys got some wheels. I admire the athleticism."

"What did he do after we left?" Manny asked.

"They tried to run after you. But with the water spilling on them and Ms. Kowalski standing in their way, you guys got such a big head start that they gave up pretty quickly. They got mad at me for spilling the water and tried to take out their anger on me. Ms. Kowalski squashed it and kicked them out. I waited for a while before I bounced."

"What about the investigation?" Uko asked.

"I had what I needed. That lady installing stuff on the computer got me thinking, so I figured I'd try a different angle. Ended up coming to school extra early today and took a trip to the principal's office."

"The principal's office? You trying to get yourself in trouble?"

"Not as long as you go early. Mr. Walker doesn't get in until around 7:30 or 8 AM. I got here at 7 AM, and his assistant let me into his office. I told her I wanted to surprise him with chocolates for putting me on the Honors List at the end of last year."

"And that worked?" both Uko and Many said simultaneously.

"Ms. Kim may be his assistant, but she loves me! Plus, I gave her some of the chocolates, so I was golden. Anyway, I get inside and look around. Mr. Walker didn't leave anything interesting on his desk, his file cabinets were locked, and his trash bin was empty. But!" Brandon said unnecessarily loudly for effect before leaning in, "his bookshelf had an old Post-It note with what looked like it might be his computer password on it. I test it out, and thankfully that was it. I log in, I look around, and I see the same icon on his desktop that I saw that lady pull up when she was installing that program in the computer lab. I open it up and it pulls up a bunch of boxes that look like TV screens. Each one has a different teacher name on them. There's a box that says Mr. Santiago, one for Mrs. Lamar, a Ms. Fielder, and a Mr. Kemp box."

"Ohhhh, the teachers on the laptop list," Manny said with surprise.

"Exactly," Brandon replied. "So, I'm staring at these boxes and all of them are pitch black except one—Mr. Kemp. His box is blurry, but I can see that it's a picture of a chalkboard. So I sit down and I stare at it. I'm trying to figure out what's so special about a chalkboard. Then, out of nowhere, the camera shakes and Mr. Kemp sits down in front of it—like we were doing a Facetime or something."

"Word? Did he see you?" Uko asked.

"I don't know. I closed the program really quickly and bounced. Almost forgot to leave the chocolates."

"What do you think that was?" Manny asked.

"I'm not sure. But it's something. I gotta figure it out. We're getting close," Brandon replied. "If you wanna get your name on this story, you boys better find something before I crack the whole thing by myself."

Without saying goodbye, he left Manny and Uko and walked into the school. They could hear the loud ringing of the bell that warned students they had five minutes to get to homeroom. They began their walk into the school.

"Maybe we snoop around after school today," Uko suggested.

"Can't today. I'm meeting up with Adriana," Manny replied.

"Oh yeah?"

"It's not that serious. It's mainly just working on campaign stuff since she's helping me run for class president. That's what I was gonna tell you if we had a chance to talk in the car."

"Oh. My bad," Uko said. "I didn't know you guys were talking like that."

"We exchanged numbers. We spoke a while on the phone last night. She's really cool." Manny smiled and nodded awkwardly.

Uko didn't know what else to add. His best friend was hanging out with an 8th grader, and Uko had been too busy talking about his dreams to find out. He felt silly. And childish. And jealous. He recognized the look that Manny had when he described spending time with Adriana. It was how Uko looked whenever he would describe some dream with Toni when he was first becoming a Nightmare Detective. The difference was that those were dreams, and this was real. Manny was going to spend time with Adriana today, and the last time Uko had seen Toni, it was the middle of the summer.

"But you said you were going to help with my campaign, right?" Manny said. "Maybe you can come too if you're not busy."

Uko knew he wasn't busy. He'd just suggested looking around the school. But no one wants to be the third wheel. So as the boys got to the noisy school hallway on their way to homeroom, he decided to lie. "I just remembered that I have to do something with Femi after school. Maybe some other time."

"Okay. Cool," Manny replied. His face looked like he didn't believe what he'd just heard. But he didn't say anything else. Instead, they walked through the crowded hallway in silence till they got to homeroom.

The boys didn't talk much as they sat and listened to Ms. Givens do roll call. Instead they put their bookbags on their desks and mindlessly played with zippers and loose strings. Uko thought about what these campaign hangouts between Manny and Adriana were like. He wondered if she was funny, or if she thought Manny was funny. *What do they talk about? Probably not just school president stuff*, Uko thought. *Manny probably talks to her about everything. Maybe they talk about me. Is it conceited to wonder if they talk about me?*

"Uko, you have Mr. Kittles after homeroom today, right?" Ms. Givens asked as she broke his concentration.

"Yes."

"Right. He asked if you could get to his class as soon as homeroom is over. He wanted to discuss an assignment with you."

"He giving you extra work?" Manny leaned over and asked. Uko shrugged.

When the bell for homeroom rang, Uko grabbed his things and nodded a quick goodbye to Manny, heading out of the door before any of the other students. He jogged down the hall and got to Mr. Kittle's class as the last student from his homeroom group of 7th graders walked out.

"You wanted to see me?"

"Hey Uko, come in. Have a seat," Mr. Kittles replied when he looked up from the textbook he was reading. Uko walked over and sat at a desk in front of his. "How are you doing?" Mr. Kittles asked as Uko got settled.

"I'm doing all right."

"Just all right?"

"I guess. Getting used to the new school and all of that."

"You not having issues with our friend Simms, are you?"

The embarrassing thought of running out of Coding Club came to Uko, and he couldn't bring himself to repeat the story. He decided that he would bring it up if something else came up between them. "No. I think we're good. I'll figure it out."

Mr. Kittles stared at Uko as he spoke, as if he were reading his eyes instead of listening to what he said. "You don't have to say that. If you need help, you can tell me. I told your dad that I got you. I meant that."

Uko looked down at his desk. What gave it away? he thought. "Thanks, Mr. K. I guess it's not going that great. He came into Coding Club while me and Manny were there. He came with a bunch of friends and pretended they wanted to join. As soon as they got in, they sat right behind us and started mean mugging."

"Did you tell Ms. Kowalski?"

"No. We just ran out. I should have said something, but I got too scared. Maybe they weren't going to doing anything at all. Maybe they just wanted to mess with me. Now that we ran and they know I'm scared, it's gonna be worse. I don't know what's gonna happen after school today. And Manny's hanging out with this girl Adriana, so it'll just be me." As Uko said those last words, he felt a wave of loneliness. His eyes tingled with the sensation of held-back tears forcing their way out. He tilted his head to the ceiling hoping gravity would keep them in. "I just want to enjoy middle school and nothing's working."

"It's okay to cry, Uko." Mr. K said as he got up from his desk. "Let it out."

Uko lowered his gaze, gravity let go, and the tears flowed. He used the back of his hand to wipe what he could.

"This is a big transition, and you got a lot going on," Mr. K added.

Uko had never felt so raw and open in front of a teacher before. He couldn't believe Mr. K was giving him permission to unload. "I had it all figured out last year. Now I'm here, and I got to start all over. I feel like a kid dealing with grown-up problems and it's not fair. Even Pangea's completely different." Uko caught himself before saying more. He wiped some more tears and calmed down a bit.

"Did you say Pangea?"

"Huh?" *Ugh*, he heard that.

Mr. K didn't repeat himself. Instead he read Uko's eyes again. "I've heard a story like this before. I remember I wrote it down." Mr. K stared at Uko as he continued. "In my notebook. The Oral History of Pangea. I forget which volume."

Uko's head jerked up with a loud and wet sniffle. Mr. K smiled.

"You're the Griot?"

"Not THE Griot. But I'm one of them. You couldn't leave such an important job to just one person."

Every worry or regret or pang of loneliness was pushed by a tsunami of astonishment. Uko's red and puffy eyes opened wide, and Mr. K chuckled in response.

"I am a Griot of Pangea," Mr. K continued. "We're a proud bunch."

Uko couldn't believe his ears. "So you know about Pangea. You know that it's real."

"Of course. It's special. That's why I do what I do. The name Griot comes from a tradition in African villages. The Griot was in charge of learning the entire history of the village—the people, the wars, the festivals, the myths. He or she would share that history in stories they'd recite for the other villagers. Before they died, they had to teach everything they knew to the next generation. Imagine keeping the history textbook of where you're from in your head."

"Dope."

"That tradition lives on in Pangea. Hundreds of people around the world speaking with the citizens of Pangea and documenting their stories. One day there'll be an entire wing in a museum dedicated to volumes of The Oral History."

Uko's heart filled with joy at the thought. "Do you have any more?"

Before Mr. Kittles could reply, the first group of students for the next period came into class. They noisily took their seats and said hello to Mr. K.

"We'll talk later. Take your seat, Uko. Let's get started," Mr. Kittles said. "Come by after school. We'll talk more Pangea. Since you're free and lonely and sad and in need of a friend," he added with a small laugh.

Uko laughed back and went to his seat.

The rest of the school day flew by. Uko did his best to concentrate, but every free moment was consumed by thoughts of Pangea and his favorite teacher being a major part of it. He spent fourth period trying to decide which Detective story he would tell. Sixth period was dedicated to remembering his run-ins with Chief and imagined conversations where Mr. K marveled at Uko's bravery. When school officially ended, Uko rushed to get his things before heading back to Mr. Kittles' classroom.

"There you are," Mr. Kittles said as he arrived. "Let's head to the teacher lounge. I got some quizzes to grade."

"Cool."

It took longer to get to the lounge than expected because of the amount of times Mr. K stopped to say hello or share a joke with a teacher or student that passed by. Uko knew that the school loved him, but he didn't realize it was this deep. When they finally got to the teacher's lounge, Uko made sure to savor being in the lounge for the first time ever. He wasn't sure how many people it would impress, but he was sure that students in the lounge were not a common occurrence. The room was a little larger than a class, with a few tables for teachers, a microwave, and a coffee machine in the corner. There were two teachers at a table that stopped their conversation when they noticed Mr. K and Uko enter the room. Uko noticed that one of them was Mr. Kemp, an 8th grade teacher that was on the laptop list that Brandon had been obsessing over.

Mr. K dropped his stack of quizzes on a table near the door and took a seat with Uko.

"What you got, Kittles?" the teacher that Uko didn't know asked.

"Quizzes."

"Wait till you start your first 8th grade class next year and they got you preppin' these kids for NESPOP exams," Mr. Kemp said with disgust in his voice. "No money for decent textbooks, but if they don't pass these district tests, I'm the one who gets fired."

"Crazy," Mr. K replied with little enthusiasm before he turned to Uko, rolled his eyes, and whispered, "Always complaining."

Mr. Kemp and the other teacher went back to their conversation and the papers they were working on. Mr. K began grading his quizzes.

"So what's Pangea like for you?" Mr. K asked.

"It's cool. I'm a Nightmare Detective."

Mr. K picked his head up. "A Nightmare Detective? Look at you. Nice!"

It felt both weird and incredibly satisfying to get recognition for being a Detective from someone while awake.

"I couldn't get into jumping into stressful dreams like that," Mr. K added. "Much respect. That's not easy work."

"Thanks. It's wild that you know about it. I've spent my whole summer trying to convince my boys about it, and they pretty much just humor me. They're probably wondering when I'll go full-on crazy."

Mr. K laughed loudly, causing Mr. Kemp and the other teacher to look back with annoyed expressions. "Sorry," Mr. K said to them.

"Is he gonna be staying here?" Mr. Kemp asked while looking at Uko. "Don't remember this being a student lounge," he added, looking directly at Uko. "You don't have anywhere to be? School's out, ain't it?"

"He's good," Mr. K responded before Uko could. "We won't be loud again."

"It's not just about y'all being loud," Mr. Kemp responded. "How do you know we're not working on stuff he's not supposed to be listening to?"

"He'll close his ears then."

The other teacher tapped Mr. Kemp on the shoulder to get him to drop the argument and turn back around. He grunted and turned back to their work.

Mr. K shook his head and turned to Uko. "So annoying. Like he's doing legit work anyway."

"What do you mean?" Uko asked. He leaned closer, afraid that Mr. Kemp was listening to them.

Mr. K stared at the backs of the teachers for a moment and then looked at Uko. "If you're gonna cheat, then why are you complaining? You can't do both."

"What?" Uko asked. He thought he must have heard wrong.

Mr. K leaned closer. "Maybe I shouldn't be saying this, but I'm sure you'll hear it at some point. Because if it's a secret, then it's the most poorly kept one I've ever seen."

Uko's mouth hung open for a second before he could form his question. "Mr. Kemp's students are cheating on their district exams?"

"Not the students. Mr. Kemp is cheating," Mr. K replied. "And he's not the only teacher."

CHAPTER 22

It's Go Time

"Are you serious?" Uko asked. "How do you know?"

Mr. K sucked his teeth and looked back at his quizzes. "It's a sloppy operation. I'll put it that way."

"Why hasn't anyone done anything about it?"

"Good question. I ask myself the same thing. Maybe the administration sees the results and pretends they don't know how it's happening," Mr. K replied. "Wouldn't be surprised." He looked at Uko's face—the complete opposite of 'not surprised.'

"There's such a thing as doing the right thing the wrong way," he added. "Keep your eyes open, and you'll see it happen more often than you think."

Uko nodded his head and tried to let this revelation sink in. This had to be the big story that Brandon had been looking for. Now Uko was gonna be the one to crack it. He thought about what it would be like to see his name on the blog and the excitement that would come from exposing a teachers' scandal.

"Let me mind my business," Mr. K said, shaking his head. "Tell me about being a Nightmare Detective. Have you done anything interesting? Met anyone crazy?"

Uko grinned. He would normally be vague in discussing Pangea with the Council. Unless he absolutely needed their help on something, he avoided getting into conversations about the ins and outs of his dream life. Since they could never experience it with him, there was always a disconnect.

Uko opened up and told him everything he could remember about his time in Pangea. He talked about Toni and the pain of missing her. He talked about meeting Chief. He talked about his time at the Isle of the Dead and crossing paths with Nasir. He talked about his experience with the Oracle and his new mission to destroy Chief. Time melted away as he talked and talked. Mr. K graded quizzes as he listened to the beginning of the story but by the end, he had his entire attention on Uko. It was clear that Mr. K didn't expect to hear all of this when he asked Uko to open up about Pangea. By the time Uko finished, it was after 5 PM and the only other person in the lounge with them was a janitor cleaning out a trashcan.

"That's wild," Mr. K finally said. "I gotta write this down in my notebook when I get a chance. You've seen both Chief and the Oracle face-to-face? Incredible."

Uko nodded with pride. "I know, right?"

"Right," Mr. K chuckled. He looked at his watch and noticed the time. "Wow, look at that. Gotta go." He began packing his papers. "Do you need a ride?"

"Yes, please. Thank you."

"No worries."

Mr. Kittles' car was pretty messy when Uko stepped into the passenger seat. There were books, loose papers, a football, and other random items that needed to be thrown into the back to make room for him. When they were finally settled and on the road, Mr. Kittles cracked the window open to let in the breeze and city sounds of the fall evening.

"That stuff I told you about Mr. Kemp cheating on those tests—don't repeat that to other people. I don't want you getting yourself into something."

"Okay," Uko said. "Who are the other teachers doing the cheating? Are Ms. Fielder or Mrs. Lamar in on it too?"

Mr. K shot Uko a suspicious glance. "So you're the type to just pretend to not know what's going on."

"Is that a yes?" Uko asked.

"I can neither deny nor confirm."

That means yes.

"The most important thing is that you listen to what I said about not telling people," Mr. K added. "I'm serious."

"Yup."

"Okay, cool."

"You never told me what Pangea is like for you," Uko said as he stared out of the window. "I spent the whole time talking about myself."

"Don't apologize for that. You had an insane story. Never apologize for your story," Mr. K responded. "My time in Pangea is nowhere near as interesting. I've met a ton of people. For the most part, I write it all down in my notebook. Try and preserve their memories in case we never meet again. Maybe one day I'll have a son or a daughter, and I'll get the chance to tell them about Pangea. I can give them my notebooks."

"That would be awesome," Uko replied. "I hope they get to experience it the same way we do. It would suck if they couldn't."

"Yeah, I hope so too. But if not, at least they can say Dad had a great imagination."

They both chuckled. Uko pointed to his house as the car approached his block.

"It was cool hanging out, Uko. I got pretty much none of my grading done. But I did get a great entry to add to the books. You don't mind if I write about you in it, do you?"

"No, it's fine."

"Great. All right, I'll let you go," Mr. K replied. "Good luck with everything."

"Thanks." Uko stepped out and walked to his house. When he got in, both his parents and Femi were all busy with their respective work. Femi was at the kitchen table finishing up homework, while his parents sat on opposite ends of the couch typing away at their laptops. Uko said hi, his family replied with a distracted hello, and he walked upstairs to his room.

He checked his phone for messages—nothing.

He pulled up his group text with Manny and Brandon and typed:

Guess what I found out today? Mr. Kemp has been cheating on the NESPOP exams! I don't know details, but I got an inside source to tell me. I think the other teachers on the list have too. Not sure how to prove it, but that's something right?!?!

As he prepped for bed later that evening, he thought about his conversation with Mr. K and the satisfaction of being able to talk about Pangea so freely with someone else. By the time he laid in bed, he had replayed their talk and the various facial expressions Mr. K made as he got to a new plot twist.

His phone chimed with a reply to the group from Brandon:

BRUH!! That's insane! I knew you'd have the big scoop. I'm all over this.

Uko threw a silly fist pump in the air as celebration. Today was a good day. Not only had he learned some pretty interesting gossip, he'd gained a better appreciation for his time in Pangea. Even if there wasn't anyone to believe his experiences, he didn't have to feel bad for having them.

With a yawn and his last bit of energy, he repeated Mr. K's words.

"Never apologize for your story."

Uko woke to the most noise and commotion he'd ever experienced in his normally peaceful dream limbo. The second he appeared, there were four or five people standing around him. There was a startled jolt from everyone as they recognized it was Uko. When they did, they immediately spoke into walkie-talkies that they carried. Everyone spoke incredibly quickly.

"Uko's here."

"He's here."

"We're clear. Uko has arrived. Going back to patrol."

Uko was so confused, he considered trying to wake up and go back to sleep again. He must be in the wrong place. Just then, a young girl walked up to him and extended her hand.

"Uko? My name's Leah. It's an honor to meet you," she said as Uko cautiously shook her hand.

"What is all of this? Why's everyone here?" Uko replied.

"Sorry about this. I wish we had a way to warn you ahead of time. We've been assigned to protect you while you're in Pangea. The dream limbo is a prime spot for Coyotes to attack unsuspecting people. So Nasir and Mel wanted to have a crew that stayed here 24/7 to make sure nothing happened to you when you went to sleep. This really is such a beautiful place," Leah responded.

Uko looked around at what used to be a silent and motionless garden. There were people of all ages walking around in patrols, looking behind trees and speaking in pairs. He felt like he was a president watching his Secret Service in action.

"I'll escort you to your Silk Road and I can answer your questions. I'm sure you've got a million. I'm new though, so I might not be helpful," she said and laughed. They began walking toward the forest. As they passed people, they would nod or smile at Uko. One man raised a fist and yelled something that Uko didn't understand.

"What happened with everyone? Mel and Christopher and everyone else?" Uko asked. "The last time I saw them, we were trying to recruit people in Yomi."

"Everybody's fine. The Yomi recruiting went well. A lot of the people here are from Yomi, like me. We heard about what you guys are trying to do and figured that helping was worth the risk. Mel and Bronson and the others have recruited more people, and they're out doing their thing. That's why we need to have security around you."

"What do you mean doing their thing?"

"The war has started, Uko," Leah said a little more gravely. "Coyotes and Nightmare Detectives are clashing all over Pangea. Some people are looking for Chief. Others are pushing back in places where the Coyotes had control. It's go time."

Uko's steps slowed as he took the news in.

"No one knows how long this will take. But we're here for it. It's gotta be done," Leah continued. They reached the edge of the forest. There were less people patrolling, but Uko did notice Christopher standing at the beginning of the Silk Road path. Christopher nodded at the two of them, and Uko returned it. As Leah turned to walk away, Uko stopped her.

"Why did you join? Have the Coyotes ever done something to you?"

Leah looked at Uko with sincere eyes as she replied, "Not directly. But evil anywhere effects everyone everywhere. In some way or another. Good luck." She spoke into her walkie-talkie and marched off.

"I know this has gotta feel weird, right?" Christopher asked.

"That's an understatement. We going to find the rest of the group?"

"The group's off doing different things, so we're not gonna be joining them yet. Nasir's deep undercover getting Gumshoe Detectives, since they're supposed to be the spies of this whole operation. We probably won't speak to him face-to-face for a while. Chef Flores and Bronson are on a mission, I forget where. Mel's looking for Chief's hideout. And I'm here with you."

"What's our mission gonna be?"

"Nothing right now. They want us to keep doing what we normally do in Pangea until they give us the word," Christopher replied. "Said they want to see how the Coyotes react. So that means we're breaking up nightmares, I guess. Detective tag team."

"That's Nasir's plan?"

"It's more than just Nasir. There's an entire group of people coming up with plans for how we do things. Everyone wants to make sure that this works, so there's a lotta chefs in the kitchen right now," Christopher replied.

"If the war started, then we should be out there, right? It feels weird to just pretend that nothing's going on."

"I don't make the rules. I'm sure we'll all link up soon."

Uko took an aggravated deep breath and weighed the few options he had. "All right, whatever. Let's go."

Uko took the lead as he and Christopher traveled the slowly darkening Silk Road on the way to the center of the forest. He imagined huge battles between Detectives and Coyotes with lasers and explosions. The type you see in a great action movie. But instead of being in the middle of that, he was stuck here doing the same old, same old.

When they reached the pitch-black middle of the forest and the end of the Silk Road, the familiar billowing fog of Uko's DreamHub poured down from the tops of the trees. Uko stared at the blurred images with little enthusiasm. After scanning for a bit, he saw a blotch with what looked like one crowd of people wrestling with another. He couldn't be certain, but he had a feeling this might be the war he so desperately wanted to be a part of. He reached out his hand to touch it and yanked it back when Christopher's voice barked out of the darkness.

"Stop! You know we can't do that one. How about the one next to it with the dolphin?"

Uko looked over at the peaceful shadow of a fish jumping out of water in front of what looked like a boat.

"Ugh! Whatever," he said as he reached out to grab it. As the fog began swirling, he saw Christopher's hand reach out toward it as well.

The flash of bright white light gave way to the ripples of the ocean. Uko and Christopher were rocking back and forth on the deck of a boat. They stood by stairs that led to what might be a small control room above the deck. It had been a while since Uko jumped into someone's nightmare and practiced the art of understanding his surroundings as quickly as possible. He was a little rusty, and the bobbing of the boat didn't help. Christopher was the first to notice the three other people, all kids their age, sitting on the edge of the boat.

"Hey, guys!" he called out.

They jumped a little, startled. "Who are you?" one of the three replied. The girl, a short redhead with oversized sunglasses, stepped off the boat's edge and approached them. She spoke calmly, but her face looked extremely worried.

"My name's Uko, and this is Christopher. We thought you guys needed some help. Is everything all right?" Uko asked. He'd learned that he didn't need to explain himself as much as he'd thought he would when entering a dream. People tend to just accept that weird things will happen. A random person appearing on a boat you were just on by yourself didn't seem too out of the ordinary.

"We don't see our friend Jesse. He was swimming with this dolphin and then we lost him," the girl replied. She pointed towards the horizon in the same direction the others on the deck's edge were staring. "We still see the dolphin. But he's gone."

"Look!" one of the other kids yelled out. He was pointing at a large boat that had appeared on the horizon and was speeding toward them. "Another boat. They can help us."

"HELP!" the other two boys on the deck yelled out. The girl walked over and joined them as everyone waved their arms furiously. "HELP!"

Christopher just stared at the boat as it got closer and closer to them. Two more boats, one on each side, suddenly appeared on the horizon. All three were barreling toward them at top speed.

Christopher spoke to Uko without taking his eyes off the boats. "Something's not right."

"HELP!" the kids kept repeating.

"Why?" Uko asked, completely confused at what Christopher was seeing that he wasn't. "What is it?"

Christopher didn't reply. Instead he pulled something from his waistband. Before Uko could get a good look at it, Christopher pointed into the area and a bright flare shot up. It soared several feet into the area and exploded in a bright cloud like a powerful firecracker.

"What the heck!" one of the boys screamed out as they covered their ears and looked back at Uko and Christopher.

"What is that?" Uko asked.

Christopher finally turned to Uko. "Something's off about those boats. I think they're Coyotes."

CHAPTER 23

She Said No

"HEEELLLLLPPPPPP!!!!!"

Christopher quickly scanned the boat before yelling orders to Uko. "Look for something you can fight with! Either that or make a weapon."

Uko's mind raced as he looked around. There were only fishing rods and coolers. As he turned to the control room for ideas, the door flew open. Bronson's massive frame squeezed out of it with surprising ease. He spotted Uko and Christopher and yelled out to them.

"Hello, boys! Got your signal. What's the problem?" He handed Uko a massive gun that looked like an oversized bazooka from a cartoon. It was so heavy it nearly smashed his feet when it slipped from his hands and smacked onto the deck.

"We got Coyotes," Christopher replied.

"What?" Bronson said. "So quick? How did they know?"

"We probably got a leak," Christopher said.

"Dang it! Nasir said this might happen."

"What are we gonna do?" Uko finally managed to ask after getting the bazooka off the ground and firmly into his arms.

"What are you guys doing?!" one of the kids screamed as the group turned around. Uko saw that Bronson was effortlessly raising his own bazooka and aiming it at the boats as they closed in.

"We're gonna fight," Bronson replied. He turned to Uko with an ear-to-ear smile that you would expect to see on someone listening to their favorite song. "Don't be precious with those shots either, darling. Let that thing fly."

Uko looked at Christopher and saw him with an identical bazooka on his shoulder, aimed in the same direction.

"Don't shoot!!" one of the kids screamed.

BOOM

The sound of Bronson's bazooka firing was deafening. Everyone stumbled back as the shot sent a massive fireball across the ocean. It seemed to travel in slow motion toward the boat before landing in the water between two of them. It missed.

A moment later, there was a loud explosion and a burst of water shot into the air. The boats rocked and stopped moving. Everything went completely still.

"Why did you do that?!" one of the kids yelled. "Who are you, anyway?"

Before anyone could say anything, another blast rang out. Uko turned to see the flash of a smaller fireball leaving one of the boats and barreling toward them. He ducked just in time as the fireball flew over his head and struck the control room of the boat. It immediately burst into flames.

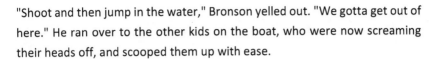

"Shoot and then jump in the water," Bronson yelled out. "We gotta get out of here." He ran over to the other kids on the boat, who were now screaming their heads off, and scooped them up with ease.

Uko summoned all his strength and yanked the bazooka up to his shoulder. He stared into the scope and pulled the trigger as hard as he could. The blow was somehow louder than Bronson's, and it pushed him further back. He felt the heat of the control room's flames as he scrambled to his feet. When he did, he saw that his shot was on target. The largest boat was on fire.

"Shoot them! Now!" Uko heard someone behind him scream. With the commotion, he was the only person on the boat to hear the cry—even though Bronson and Christopher were only an arm's length away and closer to the voice than him. Uko turned to see who it came from and couldn't believe his eyes. Over Bronson's shoulder with a large gun raised to his eye as he aimed, Chief stood tall. Next to him was the woman who had yelled the command to shoot. Her finger was outstretched toward Bronson's back, pointing him out for Chief's blast.

"Bronson!" Uko instinctively yelled. With wild eyes, Bronson turned in time to push himself over the side of the boat a split second before Chief's gun rang out.

"You idiot!" Chief bellowed at the woman next to him. "You warned them!" He turned the gun toward her as she put up her hands to protect herself. His anger with his accomplice spared Uko from being the next target.

"Jump," Christopher yelled as he tumbled over the edge of the boat. Uko followed him and jumped off. Before he hit the water, Uko heard the bang from Chief's gun go off again—followed by a scream of pain from the woman.

Another flash of white light and Uko found himself sitting on the porch of an unknown house. Next to him Christopher and Bronson were sitting on chairs on the porch, all of them soaking wet. In front, sprinklers watered a suburban lawn surrounded by a white picket fence. The sidewalk and street of the cul-de-sac they were on was completely empty.

"We're still wet," Uko said.

"Happens sometimes when you jump around. We'll be dry in a second," Christopher replied in a tired voice that sounded defeated. "I can't believe they figured out where we were so quickly."

"Probably a mole in the dream limbo crew. Wouldn't be surprised if the Coyotes got someone in there who told them the second you fell asleep and appeared in the limbo," Bronson replied. "Gonna have to replace that whole unit. Can't be too safe."

"Really?" Uko asked.

"Unfortunately," Bronson replied. "This is deeper than you thought, ain't it?"

"Yeah, I guess so. Christopher said Nasir's undercover building the Gumshoe Detectives," Uko said.

Bronson put a finger to his mouth before looking around to ensure they were truly alone. "Might want to avoid talking about that. Never know who's listening."

"Right," Uko replied. He couldn't help but feel a little overwhelmed. "It feels like there's a million of them and only a couple of us."

"We're getting our numbers up," Bronson replied. "To be fair, we're mainly replacing the people we've lost."

"What?" Uko asked. "People have died?"

"It's a war, Uko," Bronson said quietly.

"Anyone from Yomi?" Uko asked, remembering the risk they had of never waking up.

Bronson solemnly shook his head yes. Uko looked away.

"We all know what we signed up for," Christopher added after a few moments of silence.

"If you have anyone in mind, let me know," Bronson added with a forced laugh. "We're always hiring."

Uko's thoughts immediately shifted to Toni. If there was one person he'd want by his side in the middle of all of this, it was her. He wondered if she'd accept the risks that everyone else seemed to be okay with. He remembered her fighting spirit. She'd be on the frontlines.

"Maybe one of the Gumshoes can find Toni. Ask her if she wants to join," Uko asked timidly.

"That's the person who recruited you to be a Detective, right?" Christopher asked. Uko nodded.

"She's from Savannah, right? Pretty smile, tough as nails?" Bronson added.

"Yeah, that's her. Have you met her?" Uko asked. His heart swelled.

"Yeah. Nasir said you wanted us to reach out to her," Bronson replied.

"You have?!" Uko yelled. He jumped to his feet, overcome with excitement.

"Yeah, we asked if she wanted to join the cause," Bronson replied.

"WHAT DID SHE SAY?!" Uko shouted. He couldn't pretend to be calm and collected. In his mind's eye, he could see Bronson towering over her as he asked for her help. She would have some witty reply about Uko being obsessed with her. Then she'd say that she would have to clear her busy schedule, but if Uko really needed her THAT badly then—

"She said no," Bronson said as delicately as he could. "Said she didn't believe in all of this as much as she did before."

Uko had never been punched in the stomach before, but he was certain this was what it must feel like. His heart, swollen with expectation just seconds before, felt like it physically hurt. He dropped into his seat and looked back out at the chopping sprinklers. Burning tears pricked his eyes again. He didn't try to fight them.

"I'm sorry, bro," Christopher finally said.

"She wished you luck," Bronson added. "It'll be all right, though. You got us."

But Uko couldn't have felt lonelier. More abandoned. All his desire to take on this Herculean task was zapped by those three words.

She said no.

"We don't have to talk about it no more," Uko finally said.

The three of them sat in silence as time slowly crawled by. Eventually things began fading. Uko began waking up. He didn't say goodbye. He didn't ask what the next steps or plans were. He didn't care. He just closed his eyes and waited to be back in his room. Alone.

The next few months crawled by for Uko. He realized that a big part of leading the fight to defeat Chief had revolved around Toni. He was sure that something as bold as what they were doing would somehow reconnect him with her. But it didn't. The fact that he'd thought it would was crushing. Part of him wanted to give up. He'd bitten off more than he could chew, and he didn't have his most trusted friend in Pangea to help. But his memory of what happened in Coding Club kept him from doing that. He'd already tried to run away from his problems with Simms, and the feeling didn't sit well. Things might not be going the way he hoped, but he would not abandon his duty.

He became even more focused on his battle against the Coyotes while everyone in his Sleep Walking life got wrapped up in their own things. His parents got even more busy with work, Brandon chased lead after lead in his search for the school scandal, and Manny spent more and more time with Adriana. Uko preferred to spend his awake time strategizing as he filled notebooks with ways to find Chief.

There were new people stationed in his dream limbo now. Apparently Leah, the girl he met that first night, was the mole. Uko overheard someone talk about how she'd alerted the Coyotes to his presence the second he walked onto his Silk Road. So the group was replaced—more than once. There was so much paranoia in the entire process. Uko never spoke to Nasir directly. Instead, Bronson would relay messages. Nasir didn't want to blow his new disguise by being seen with Uko, so his circle was incredibly tight. He trusted no one and took every precaution. Despite this, his ranks of Gumshoe Detectives continued to get infiltrated by Coyotes pretending to be good guys. Nasir and his group were relatively new to the spy game. The Coyotes had people who had been doing this for years, and it showed. For every big step forward in the search for the Coyote hideout or the true location of Chief, there would be two steps back. The Coyotes seemed to know every move they planned before they acted, and it kept everyone on edge.

Despite that, both the Gumshoe and Nightmare Detectives continued to grow. There was still a strong enough hatred for the Coyotes in Pangea to keep a steady stream of people wanting to join. With the age restriction removed, the Nightmare Detectives seemingly doubled in size. When Uko jumped dreams in search of nightmares related to the Coyotes, he always had three or four people by his side. It was weird getting used to at first, but Uko eventually learned how to maximize the extra hands. After the first two weeks, he had a network of Detectives over all of Pangea, jumping dreams and giving him updates on what they found. If there were Coyotes in a person's nightmare, they found Uko so he could join them in the fight. It was a well-oiled machine.

The Gumshoe Detectives evolved as well and developed a ranking system. The established spies, the ones whose dedicated service earned them the trust of Nasir and Bronson, were referred to as Gumshoe 1st Class. When Uko took strolls around his limbo's garden, he heard people talk about them in hushed voices full of reverence. The goal was to move up the ranks from new Gumshoe to Gumshoe 2nd class and eventually earn that 1st Class honor.

From time to time, people would approach Uko and introduce themselves with their ranking. One night, as he sat on one of the garden's many logs, a group of three imposing women walked up to him. They were all much taller than him, with scarves that covered their faces and left only their eyes and foreheads visible. As Uko looked up at them, they saluted in perfect synchrony. It seemed so official. One of them spoke with an assertive tone.

"Commander, I am Natasha. This is Comrade Ina, and this is Comrade Phoenix. Gumshoes 1st Class."

Uko nodded awkwardly. He never felt like he deserved this level of admiration, so it was always so weird trying to decide how to respond.

"I thought you would have won this for us by now, Commander?" another voice called out from behind the wall of women. They stepped to the side to reveal a young man dressed similarly. As he walked up, he pulled his scarf down to expose his bearded face. It took a second for recognition, but Uko eventually realized who it was.

"Nasir?"

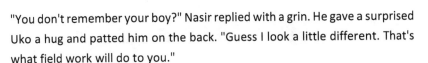

"You don't remember your boy?" Nasir replied with a grin. He gave a surprised Uko a hug and patted him on the back. "Guess I look a little different. That's what field work will do to you."

"Yeah, crazy different," Uko replied. "What are you doin' here? I thought we're never supposed to be seen together. I run the Nightmare Detectives and you run the Gumshoes from the shadows and all of that."

Nasir's escorts turned their back to the boys and began surveying the garden.

"Heard that your people have been doing good work," Nasir replied. "Coyotes are pretty much in hiding right now since they know Detectives are on the hunt. Well done, my guy."

"Thanks, man. I appreciate it."

"No problem. But there was also something else I wanted to chop it up with you about," Nasir replied.

"You need my help with the Gumshoes. I heard it's been rough for y'all."

"Don't do me like that. My job is harder than yours."

"Is it?"

Nasir snickered. "Follow me. I wanna show you something in your DreamHub. I know you're a busy man. You don't have to do anything after that. Just come check this out," Nasir said.

"Okay."

As Nasir and Uko began their walk, the Gumshoes trailed them on all sides.

Uko stared at him and his ninja scarf as they walked.

"How's it going for you guys for real?" Uko asked. As much as he'd heard about the never-ending spy games, he wasn't sure how much to believe.

"It's going. Some wins, some losses. People believe in the cause, so the momentum is on our side," Nasir replied. "How's your heart?"

Uko looked at Nasir with surprise. What an interesting question.

"It's all right. I'm focused," Uko answered. "It's good seeing you. I'm glad you're all right."

"Thanks, Commander," Nasir replied with smiling eyes. "I missed you too."

When they reached the center of the forest, the mist of the DreamHub began its familiar descent from the treetops. The purple and silver lit up the pitch-black space and reflected off of Uko, Nasir, and the escort of Gumshoes. As Uko took in the moment, he turned to his left and noticed another person standing there. He gasped as more light made the person's presence clear.

It was the Oracle, beaming like a proud grandmother.

"Hello, dear. So happy to see you," she said in her comforting voice.

"Wow," Uko replied. "What are you doing here?"

"I came to lend my support before you take your big step," the Oracle replied.

"Big step? What do you mean?" Uko asked. Nasir stepped closer to him and put his arm around his shoulder.

"We found the Coyote hideout. We found Chief," Nasir replied. Uko's mouth dropped as he turned to him. "We're a li'l better than you thought," Nasir added.

The Oracle stepped forward and placed her hands on Uko's cheeks. She smiled up at him for a moment before speaking.

"Everything's built up to this. You ready, honey?"

Uko looked at Nasir and back at the Oracle. Seeing them again for the first time in such a long while affected him more than he would have imagined. They were the reason to fight. The people who believed in him before anyone else did. His support, his friends, his day ones. They needed him now. He could only have one answer.

"Yes. Yes, I'm ready."

CHAPTER 24

Castle on a Hill

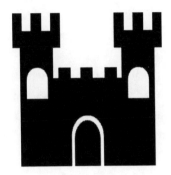

There are few things in this world that feel better than knowing your purpose.

"I knew you were ready," the Oracle replied before pinching Uko's cheek. "Godspeed to you all." She stepped back, surveyed Uko and Nasir one last time, and then turned to walk away. As she did, the forest rustled with the footsteps of several people who followed her as she walked out of the DreamHub's light and into the dark. Uko never even noticed them before she left. Everyone had security.

"Let's get this work," Nasir said as he turned to the glowing DreamHub.

Uko nodded and then turned to the DreamHub as well. "Where is he?"

"We tracked him down to this estate in the far west end of Pangea. People who know they are in Pangea stay in the cities, the places where we're most connected, where we interact with the most people. The Coyotes are on the outskirts, in the Badlands. For the people living in the Badlands, these are all just random dreams and nightmares," Nasir replied. "We've had Gumshoe double agents who have given us bad information before, but this is legit. He's there. I've triple-checked it myself."

"Cool. So what's the plan?"

"Chef Flores and the others will join us. We make our way through the Badlands as quietly as we can. Don't want to freak out the people we come across out there, so we'll keep a low profile," Nasir replied. "We make our way to the estate, get in, and take him out."

Nasir stepped to the edge of the DreamHub, where the images were dim. He reached out to a corner of it, and the fog began pooling around his arm. "Let's go," he said to Uko and the Gumshoes around them. The entire group crowded around Nasir as the fog pulled them in and the dark forest was replaced with bright white light.

◆ ◆ ◆

Dust. Dust and sand was all that Uko's squinted eyes could see. He stood in the center of a narrow dirt road with makeshift clay buildings pressing in around him. Nasir and the three Gumshoes stood next to him. They were in what looked to be a deserted village. There were clotheslines with drying shirts and dresses. In the distance, Uko saw people talking, walking, and going about their lives.

"We gotta get off the road ASAP," Nasir whispered. After the group scurried into a shadowy alley, Nasir opened the random back door of a short apartment building next to them. They squeezed in one by one, making sure they didn't draw too much attention to themselves.

"You guys go ahead and scout," Nasir said to the three Gumshoes. "Find out where the Coyotes might be while being discreet. We don't know who might be on their side. Uko and I will see what we can find."

"You got it," the tallest of the group, Comrade Ina, said in reply. The three of them pulled hoods over their heads, turned, and slipped down the hallway and out the building's front door.

"Let's make our way through. Not everyone in here has gotten into deep sleep yet. So they'll probably be in their room doing whatever they were thinking about when they fell asleep," Nasir said as he began walking. On each side of the hall was an open doorway with people inside. Every few feet, Nasir would peer into a room and decide to move to the next one for some reason known only to him. Uko looked into each of the rooms after Nasir. One man was sitting at a desk studying, while another was watching TV. They passed by a room that looked tiny on the outside but was an entire football stadium filled with fans when Uko looked in it.

After passing a few rooms, Uko heard the music from the Council's favorite video game playing from a room up ahead. After watching Nasir look in and move on, Uko turned to see who was playing City Angels IV. His heart nearly stopped when he saw Carlos, Manny, and Femi sitting around a TV with controllers in their hands. They didn't notice him as they yelled at the screen and laughed at the gameplay. Uko stood frozen to the spot.

"Uko!" Nasir yelled back at him from down the hall in his best attempt at a loud whisper. "Let's go!"

Uko couldn't hear him. The only thing running through his mind was the astonishment of actually seeing his best friends in Pangea.

It finally happened, he thought.

"Guys," he called out to them. Carlos paused the game, and the group turned to him.

"Uko?" Manny replied. "What are you doin' here?"

"I can't believe this is happening," Uko said. "You're all here."

"Why you acting weird, bro?" Femi asked.

"This is a dream," Uko replied.

"What? You act like you've never seen us before," Carlos said. "It's a dream to see us?"

"No, I mean this is an actual dream. We're all dreaming. At the same time. We're in Pangea," Uko said. Out of the corner of his eye he could see Nasir speaking with someone who had stepped into the hall.

"What are you talking about?" Manny asked.

"Don't start with this dreamworld stuff," Carlos added.

"I'm serious," Uko said. "Think about it. How did you get to this room? Do you remember walking here, or can you only remember being in this room? As if you just appeared here?"

Femi's face changed as he thought about this.

"What room is this?" Uko asked the group. "It looks like a combo of my room, Manny's room, and your basement. Isn't that weird?"

The group looked around. Uko made them notice the same things he'd seen when he first walked in. All around them were items from each of the rooms that Uko had mentioned.

"Oh snap," Carlos whispered as he looked around. "He's right."

"UKO!" Nasir screamed from down the hallway. Uko turned to see him push two people back into their room as more people began sticking their heads into the hallway. "This place is filled with Coyotes. We gotta go. NOW!" Nasir added. More people appeared in the hall and began pulling at Nasir.

"Go, bro," Carlos said to Uko. He stood in the hall next to Uko along with the rest of the Council. "We said if you met us in Pangea, we'd ride. So go do what you gotta do."

Carlos, Femi and Manny sprinted down the hall. But not before playfully smacking Uko on the back of his head as they passed. The boys charged into the group that were now crowded around Nasir and began pulling them off. Uko couldn't see what was happening clearly, but there was a massive scrum in the middle of the tight hall. Nasir squeezed through the group and came charging toward him.

"Go out the back door!" he yelled to Uko. They both ran out of the door that first brought them into the building. He chased Nasir as he sprinted across the road and in between alleys. As he ran, Nasir pulled out a walkie-talkie and screamed into it. By the time Uko caught up, they were squatting behind a building and catching their breath.

"Were those your boys?" Nasir asked through gasps.

"Yeah, my best friends and my brother," Uko replied. "They always swore I made Pangea up."

"They've never seen it. That's why they're here," Nasir said after several deep breaths. "They looked out, though. The Coyotes are in a castle above this village. Bronson and 'em are gonna meet us there."

The two of them stood up and began heading toward the location Nasir suspected Chief to be. At one point, Nasir told Uko to cover his face and head. He quickly pulled on the scarf and hood that he'd created. They walked quickly, but not too quickly, to avoid drawing attention to themselves. When they finally got outside its walls, they reached a red sand cliff that arrowed into the sky.

"It's at the top of this," Nasir said to Uko, gazing at a paper he was holding.

"We're gonna climb this?" Uko asked.

"It won't be that bad," Nasir replied. Without turning back, he stuffed the paper in his pocket and began the climb up.

Uko sighed, then joined him. His clothing was replaced with the climbing gear needed for a moment like this. With less effort than he would have expected, he and Nasir clambered to the top. When they arrived, the world they'd entered was completely different from where they'd left. The village below was dry, sandy and hot, but this hilltop was full of vegetation. It was now dark with a full moon high in the sky. The wind whipped as a thunderstorm brought sheets of rain down on them. They stood in a clearing barred by a massive and ornate gate on the other side. Behind the gate was a partially lit courtyard and a winding path that led to a massive castle.

Thunder boomed, lightning flashed, and rain drenched their clothes in moments. Uko pulled the hood of the slick, black raincoat he was now wearing over his head. Nasir listened to someone speaking on his walkie-talkie for a moment before looking to Uko.

"Everyone is in position, Commander," he whispered.

Uko saw figures creep from a bush and settle near the gate. It was dark, but he could tell it was Christopher, Bronson, Mel, and Chef Flores. He was actually here, on his way to facing Chief one last time.

"You ready to have them get us in?" Nasir asked.

Uko rubbed his hands together, chasing the cold out of them. "Are you sure this is it?"

"The intelligence is rock solid. My best team was on the assignment. This is the stronghold we've been looking for."

Uko hesitated. After everything they had gone through, he worried if this was another trap. Would he be giving them the command to put themselves in danger? With conflicting feelings, he told Nasir to move forward. Nasir smiled and raised a closed fist to signal the group. They immediately began cutting a hole into the iron gate. When they finished, Nasir and Uko joined them. The group said quiet 'hellos' to each other as they came together and surveyed their surroundings.

"They probably have surveillance along the path," Nasir whispered. "It took so long for Bronson and Christopher to disable the gate's camera that it would be a waste of time to do that to any others. We just have to avoid them."

"There are some stairs back there," Uko said. He pointed at moss covered cobbled stairs hidden by the trunk of a massive tree. They led straight up toward the castle—a shortcut for those who wanted to avoid the winding path.

"Excellent. Good eye," Nasir said. "Mel, go ahead on the stairs. Scout for traps or cameras. We won't be far behind. Bronson, go with her."

She jogged up the stairs, Bronson right behind her.

Nasir knelt down and began searching the bookbag he had been carrying. "I need to keep this more organized," he said to himself.

Uko pulled his hood tighter and stared down the path in front of them. The trees cast dark shadows that made it hard to see farther than a few feet. As Uko stared, rumbles of thunder and a flash of lightning illuminated the road ahead. Uko could see the silhouette of what looked like a prowling dog walking toward them. A lump formed in his throat, and he pointed a shaky finger in its direction.

Nasir looked up from his bag, noticed Uko pointing, and looked in that direction as well. At that moment, another flash of light highlighted the animal again as it sniffed the ground and continued toward them. Nasir immediately dropped his bag and pulled the walkie-talkie from his hip, bringing it to his mouth.

"We got a sighting. Knuckle up," he whispered into it.

"Where do you see the coyote?" Mel's voice crackled back in response.

"Fifty paces ahead of us at the base of the path," Nasir replied. Christopher and Chef Flores immediately took cover in the trees nearest them. Uko's head swiveled from side to side as he tried to decide what he should do.

"Well, that came fast," Mel replied. "This is it."

Another burst of lightning flashed as the coyote leapt out from the dark path. It barreled full speed at Nasir as he continued to frantically look through his bag.

"Nasir!" Uko yelled as he stood in front of him to protect him.

Nasir yelled back at him. "Get out of the—"

Before he could finish his sentence, everything around them slowed to a crawl. The coyote was suspended in mid-air only a few feet from Uko. At the same time, Nasir was shoving Uko to the side as he raised his hand to the coyote. The slo-mo effect didn't last long. Before Uko's thoughts could catch up, everything returned to its normal speed. He heard a swishing sound by his ear as he fell. Nasir dropped to his right, and the Coyote crumpled into a pile a few feet behind them. Uko rolled onto his back, prepared for the coyote to get to its feet and charge again, but it never did. He remained in a pile of jumbled legs as Nasir walked over to Uko with a long silver gun in his hand. He showed it to Uko as he spoke.

"Tranquilizer," he said before turning to one of the trees the group was hiding behind. "Thanks for slowing things down, Chef Flores. Needed that extra second."

"No problem," Chef Flores said as she stepped out. Their conversation was cut off by the sound of Mel's voice on the walkie-talkie.

"Guys, we made it to the castle. Bronson had to shift into a coyote to get by some guards, but it's all good now. Come up the side steps we took. We cleared the path."

Nasir clapped in excitement. "Copy that. We're on our way. Good freaking job."

Nasir grabbed his bag, and the group hustled up the side steps. When they reached the top, they crouched and searched the grounds for Mel and Bronson. Even with the lightning, it was difficult to see anything clearly. The massive castle blocked the moonlight.

"Where are you guys?" Nasir whispered into his walkie-talkie.

Mel responded by flickering a flashlight from the second-floor balcony on the side of the castle. The rest of the team ran over to them, climbed up the piping that Mel had used, and joined them. They huddled around an open window.

"Climb in," Bronson said before sliding his foot into the window and entering. Everyone followed and regrouped in a hallway that was several feet above the main floor. There were no rooms on the floor they were on. Instead, it circled an opening that let you look down on a large ballroom. As they gazed down at the floor below, they saw what was causing the loud commotion. Hundreds of people stood in a large ballroom. All of them were listening to one person speak—Chief.

From the front of the ballroom, the charisma that had led hundreds to join the Coyotes was on full display. Chief paced back and forth, his deep blue and crimson dashiki flowing freely. His voice was so loud and crisp it easily carried upstairs. From time to time, he would wave his cane or strike it on the floor to emphasize his points. When he did take breaks from speaking, he glared at the audience with a menacing smile, his dark shades making it impossible to see exactly who he was looking at. Uko and the group lay on the floor and crawled to the edge so they could look down without being spotted.

"There he is. I can't believe it," Christopher whispered to Uko. "I can't believe I'm seeing him in person."

"Don't get caught up. That's what he wants everyone to do—think of him as some larger-than-life figure," Chef Flores whispered back.

"All of Pangea thinks he's a god. That he can't be killed or stopped," Nasir added. "If we cut him down in front of everybody, he loses his mystique and his power over everyone."

"Don't know how we'll do it with all those Coyotes here. But that's the plan," Mel said. "Did you hear something?"

"What?" Uko asked.

"SIR!" a voice boomed from behind the group. Christopher, Uko, Bronson, Mel and Nasir all flipped onto their backs in horror at the noise. Standing over them were three Coyotes with long blades in their hands. Another three were crawling into the balcony window that they had just entered from. "We have visitors!" The guard who yelled out their presence walked over to Uko and laid his blade on the floor next to him. He reached down and grabbed Uko's shirt to pull him onto his feet.

Before he could, Uko pulled his leg back toward his chest as far as he could. The movement caused him to bang his head against the balcony bars that kept them from falling to Chief and the Coyotes on the first floor below them. He quickly grabbed the guard's shoulders and drove his cocked-back foot into his stomach while pulling him back toward the balcony. The fluid motion launched the guard up and over the balcony and tumbling toward the congregation below. Uko was taking full advantage of the fact that if you focus well enough in Pangea, you can do almost anything.

256

Before everyone else could react, Uko scrambled to his feet and picked up the blade the guard had left next to him. He quickly looked over the balcony and spotted Chief in the crowd as everyone watched what was happening above them.

Only shot, Uko thought as he grabbed the tip of the sharp blade and threw it toward Chief as hard as he possibly could. The blade sliced through the air in furious flips toward Chief's head as everyone was frozen in surprise. At the very last moment, Chief leaned out of the blade's path and it drove itself deep into the wooden wall next to him. The crowd of Coyotes roared with delight at their leader's swift move.

"No!" Uko yelled at the near-miss. *How the heck did he avoid that?!*

Uko turned back toward the group, and a guard was right in front of him. In a split second, the guard struck Uko in the face with something so quickly, Uko did not know what it was. There was just an incredibly intense pain before everything went black.

CHAPTER 25

We Have Time

They were on display in front of the crowd of Coyotes—up on stage while tied to uncomfortable chairs so that Chief could make an example out of them. They squirmed in their seats, but it was hopeless.

"The efforts to defeat your leader were fruitless," Chief yelled out. The crowd roared. They reacted with enthusiasm to everything that Chief gave them. As he paced the stage, three Coyote henchmen—personal bodyguards—stood up front with him and kept their eyes on the crowd. "How they will bend over backwards to try and topple the good work that we are doing. I expect nothing less. I've dealt with this hatred outside of Pangea as well."

The bodyguards stood directly behind Uko and the group. Their long blades reflected the light of the torches that burned offstage. Defeat settled in his stomach. He went over the last few minutes in his head again and again. How easy would it have been to have someone keep an eye on the window?

"They left me for DEAD!" Chief continued. "This world does not care for the downtrodden. And that's what I am. I live my Waking Life as a homeless man. Not a king or a politician or the heir to some fortune. My day-to-day life is on the street. That is why I'm able to lead the Coyotes so well. I'm from the bottom like so many of you."

Homeless?

Uko looked over at the rest of the group in their chair prisons. Everyone looked just as surprised.

"This society gave me nothing," Chief said. "So I take from it, everything."

The crowd roared with applause. Chief raised his cane to the air. He sauntered over to the prisoners and stopped in front of Uko. He removed his dark shades and stared into Uko's face. "You lose again, boy," he said before turning back to the crowd.

"This one is my favorite!" Chief bellowed. He stuck his cane into Uko's chest, and he screamed in pain. "I personally, PERSONALLY invited him to join the Coyotes and he turned me down. Can you believe that?"

The crowd erupted into hisses and boos. After a few moments, Chief raised his cane for quiet.

"He thought that being a Nightmare Detective was more noble. He told me that he would defeat me. In Pangea!" Chief yelled in a mocking tone. "Can I be killed in Pangea?"

"NO!" the crowd yelled back.

"Why?" Chief yelled back.

"Because you are immortal!"

The entire crowd spoke in unison—as if they'd rehearsed it multiple times. Two of the bodyguards on stage repeated the words as well. The one standing by Uko did not.

"Now, I show you all my power by extinguishing this entire group right before your eyes," Chief said. "Give me your blade," he commanded the guard near Uko.

The crowd whipped itself into a frenzy. Everyone pushed forward to watch Uko and his crew lose their lives and be banished to the Isle of the Dead. Uko pulled at the straps holding him to his seat with all his might. It didn't do anything. Defeated, he looked over to the others on his right. Christopher, Chef Flores and Mel looked just as terrified as him. He looked to his left at Bronson and Nasir. They looked back at him with completely different expressions. They were smiling.

As Uko cocked his head to try and understand what was going on, the guard who Chief had called over pulled out his blade. The crowd screamed in anticipation. Chief turned to them and raised his arms in triumph.

The guard then thrust the blade into Chief's throat.

Someone screamed in the back of the crowd. Then everyone went perfectly silent. It was as if all the air was gone from the room as everyone stared. Chief gurgled and reached for the blade futilely before collapsing to the ground. The guard that had stabbed him crouched over Chief's body and whispered something. Even in the silence, it was too hard to hear what he said. Then Chief vanished.

The guard then stood up and pulled off the hoodie and scarf covering his face. Luscious springs of curly hair flowed freely. The guard then turned to Uko and smiled. In the baggy hoodie, Uko had assumed he was being taken in by a man or a tall boy. But the smile, the flawless skin, and the gold bracelet that flashed in the light as she fixed her hair said otherwise. Uko had imagined the girl so many times this moment felt like a dream.

Toni, standing in front of Uko and the others, was more than a dream. She was a revelation.

She handed her blade to Uko so he could cut himself free. He accepted it without breaking eye contact. He had so many simultaneous thoughts he could barely operate.

Toni then turned to the crowd that was still in stunned silence.

"Was that someone who was immortal? No! He was just like the rest of us. He just had everyone believing he was something more," she yelled out.

The other guards on stage finally recovered from their shock and approached Toni. By that point, Bronson had been cut free. At his side, he held the same oversized bazooka from the boat.

"If you want to make a difference in Pangea, you can join us. Become a Nightmare Detective. I know y'all heard that it's not just kids anymore," Toni continued. "But even if you don't want to become a Detective, you don't need to be a Coyote. You don't need to do this anymore."

A murmur rippled through the crowd as they decided what they would do. After a few moments, it parted down the middle. People stepped to either side to allow the group to leave. Everyone looked at each other to see who would take the first step forward. It could be another trap, after all.

"It's over," Nasir finally said. "Let's go." He slung his backpack over his shoulder and walked into the crowd. People stared at him, but no one did more than that. Soon Chef Flores followed along with everyone else. They opened the front doors and went back down the winding path that they had avoided on their way to the castle. No one spoke until they reached the gate.

When they finally did, Chef Flores let out a nervous laugh that was joined by a scream of excitement from Christopher. Everyone shared hugs and congratulations. The only two to not join them in the celebration was Toni and Uko. They looked at each other, unable to speak.

Toni broke the silence with a kiss on the cheek and tight hug.

"I missed you," she said.

"Me too," Uko replied. "I've been trying to find you for months. Then Bronson said he found you but that you didn't want to join us."

"That's on me, Uko," Bronson cut in. "I had to lie. She was in so deep with the Coyotes that I didn't want to risk it. But I felt really bad. When you cried, I thought about just telling you."

"You cried?" Toni asked with tears in her eyes.

"No. Ain't nobody cry," Uko replied, brushing a tear away.

Everyone laughed. Nasir walked over and stuck out his hand for Toni to shake. "Congratulations, Detective Toni. Gumshoe Detective—1st Class."

Toni ignored the hand and gave him a hug that caused him to break out in laughter. "I made it!"

"Yes, you did," Mel said. "You should be proud."

"I'm proud of all y'all," Toni responded.

"So what happens now?" Christopher asked no one in particular.

"Chief is on the Isle of the Dead. Eventually he'll make his way out. But things will be completely different for him now," Bronson replied. "He built his rep on being the one person in Pangea you couldn't touch. Now there's a chink in his armor. Not only was he killed, but he was killed by someone who got close to him. He had a traitor he wasn't even aware of. He can't command the same respect. He got taken out by a little girl."

"Little girl?" Toni asked with raised eyebrows.

"You know what I mean," Bronson said.

"Somebody will probably replace him," Nasir interrupted. "You know that, right?"

"Yeah," Uko replied. "But we'll be ready. The Detectives are strong now."

"Plus, we got the Oracle's blessing," Bronson added with a clap of his massive hands.

"That's right. That blessing does come in handy," Nasir replied.

The group exchanged stories of their adventures as they headed back to the village. They compared points and playfully corrected each other when someone tried to make themselves look braver in retrospect.

"We better stay in contact," Mel said to the group at the end of the storytelling.

"Better," Chef Flores repeated.

"No doubt," Toni said. "You're gonna stay in contact, aren't you?" she asked Uko.

"Of course," he replied. "Want to meet up at my limbo garden tomorrow night?"

"It's been a while," Toni replied. "Sounds like a plan."

❖ ❖ ❖

Uko woke up that morning in the best spirits he'd ever been in. He popped out of bed before dancing in front of the mirror on his bedroom wall. He picked up Kanju, laughed, and included his favorite stuffed lion in his victory dance. After a few minutes he ran to his phone and sent a text to Manny, Carlos and Femi. He was surprised at how quickly the replies started coming in.

UKO: Mornin' fellas. Any good dreams last night?
CARLOS: You guys were in my dream actually
MANNY: Same, you guys were in mine too
UKO: Funny how that works. I saw you guys in mine. You have the same dream too Femi?
FEMI: Nope
UKO: He's lying
FEMI: Ok, yeah I did. What's the point?
UKO: Pangea is somethin' else ain't it?

He put his phone away as he finished prepping for school. He had a lot of missed time to make up for. Months of being out of it pushed him away from friends. Now he had his spark back in a way he could have never imagined. He was so happy, he couldn't wait to see the people he had been avoiding at school—Brandon, Manny, Mr. K, even Simms.

He got ready as quickly as he could and headed to the bus stop. After coming up with excuses about why he wouldn't catch the same bus to school with Manny, Uko knew that Manny wouldn't ask him today. Instead, he decided to surprise Manny during his class president debate. The race had come down to Manny and one other kid, so today they would go head-to-head during the sixth grade assembly in the gym. Uko planned to get to school early enough to make a "Manny for President" banner that he'd hold up during the entire debate.

By the time the debate rolled around in the afternoon, Uko was prepped and ready to go. He had his posterboard covered in colorful magic marker. He kept his conversation with Manny throughout the day brief to keep him off the scent. He wanted him to be fully surprised when he became his biggest cheerleader at the assembly. As the entire sixth grade class and their teachers filed into the gym, he stood to the side of the bleachers with his board folded in two. He watched Manny on stage as he got last-minute coaching from Adriana. Then, as the principal opened the debate, she gave him a hug and sat in the first row.

"Welcome everyone, welcome to this year's sixth grade class presidential debate," Principal Walker started. "We're going to be respectful and keep our voices down as the candidates speak."

As Principal Walker went further into his speech, the sound of people in the crowd started growing.

"Quiet down everyone, this is what I'm talking about," he said loudly into the mic. "Quiet down."

But the crowd didn't get quieter. In fact, the din of conversation got louder and was now mixed with the sounds of people getting text messages. Uko watched person after person look at their phone, and then show it to the person next to them. As he started wondering what was going on, he got a text message on his phone. He checked and saw that it was a link to a post on the blog Last Word. When he opened it, he gasped.

NIGHTMARE DETECTIVE

Not One Scandal at Robeson Middle School, but Two: Teachers Being Recorded on School Issued Laptops as Principal Tries to Catch them Cheating

Written by John Henry, Anansi, and Duende

Sometimes you get two for the price of one. After multiple tips and investigative reporting, we have confirmed that there are at least four Robeson Middle School teachers who have been cheating on their students' NESPOP exams to get better scores with the district. To make things even crazier, Principal Walker has implemented a questionable method to prove it. Earlier this year, the school provided these teachers with laptops that had secret software that used its camera and microphone to spy on them in an attempt to catch them in the act...

Uko put his phone away before reading the rest. He couldn't believe that this was happening, and from the looks of the staff that were now all staring at their phones, neither did they. After being shown a phone, Principal Walker spoke into the microphone again.

"Ladies and gentleman, these debates have been postponed. Please head to your 5th period class immediately." As soon as he finished speaking, the crowd erupted in conversation. It took the effort of all of the teachers to get the students back under control.

Even though things were now much more interesting at school, the only thing that Uko could think of was going back to sleep. He rushed through the rest of his day and skipped dinner so he could get to bed as soon as possible. Since becoming a Detective, he had spent so much time thinking about what he would do if he ever connected with Toni again. Now it was real, and he was so excited, he couldn't get himself to actually close his eyes. He had so much to tell her, so many questions about what she'd done since the summer, so many ideas for hanging out in Pangea. He went through dozens and dozens of conversations in his head as he lay awake. This was everything he wanted.

267

✦ ✦ ✦

"There you are," Uko heard as soon as he appeared in his dream limbo garden. It was back to its quiet state. There were no more patrols of people making sure that he was safe; just soft breezes, butterflies, and Toni sitting quietly on a log by the campfire.

"I had some trouble falling asleep," Uko replied as he sat down next to her.

"Me too," she replied. "So how are you?"

All of Uko's ideas for conversation flew out of his mind. Now that he was actually here, he couldn't do more than stare. His mind went blank.

"I'm nice. I'm good. Fine," he stammered. "I'm fine. What about you?"
"The same. How is school?"

"School? School is all right. Getting used to sixth grade. How do you like your school?"

"It's okay, I guess. Getting used to it too."

"That's good."

"Yup."

Uko looked at the campfire in frustration. Things were not going as smoothly as he'd thought they would.

"I really missed you," he said before he could stop himself.

"Me too," she replied. "Can't believe I'm a Nightmare Detective again. Just when you retire, the Ukos of the world pull you back in."

"I'm glad it worked."

"Me too."

"I have like a million and one questions," Uko said. "And I don't wanna overwhelm you, but I just wanna know so many things about how you've been."

Toni placed her hand on his. "Don't worry about it. I'm not going anywhere. We've got time."

They both looked into the campfire.

"Till one of us wakes up at least," Uko said.

"Then we'll hang out the next night."

"Yeah."

"Maybe one day we can do it in real life," Toni added.

Uko turned to her. "You think so?"

"Hopefully," she replied. "We'll figure it out. Maybe I can convince my folks to take a family trip to New York with a stop in Jersey."

"That would be dope," Uko said. He worked hard to keep himself from overreacting at the thought. "I wrote you a letter when school started and I couldn't find you in Pangea. I couldn't mail it to you since I don't know your address."

"That's so nice. If I tell you my address, will you remember it when you wake up so you can mail it?"

"Don't need it," Uko replied.

"You don't?"

"Nope. I memorized the letter a long time ago."

Toni blushed. "Even better."

Uko looked into the campfire again and took a deep breath. He was finally calm. Pangea was safe. They had time. He started reciting the letter that he had reread so many times. It was etched in his mind.

"Dear Toni, I hope you've had an incredible summer..."

THE END

ABOUT THE AUTHOR

Monk Inyang is a Nigerian-American husband and father of two from Newark, New Jersey who enjoys creating adventures that represent the neighborhoods he grew up in. He lives in Montclair, NJ with his wife, two kids, and two cats. You can find more of his work on his website **www.monkinyang.com**

Made in the USA
Middletown, DE
07 November 2020

23507605R00168